A DRUMMER BOY FOR CHRISTMAS

Elaine Reed

Drummer Boy For Christmas

ISBN: 979-8-9871057-1-9

Published by Fabulist

Released in the United States of America

Editor: Cece Carroll, www.cececarroll.com

Cover Art and Formatting: Suzanna Chriscoe,
ElefontBooks.com

Disclaimers

Contents

CHAPTER ONE

Need to get out of the house?
Crawford's opens at 8. Merry
Christmas, Ann Arbor.

VAUGHN HIT "POST" and leaned her head on the headrest. If her Uncle Lori wasn't in the car by the time she reached "10," she was gonna lay on the horn.

Yes, it was Christmas. And yes, this was a nice, quiet neighborhood. No, she didn't care anymore. He'd been fighting with someone in the house since he'd arrived two days before. Vaughn had had enough.

6... 7...

A blast of cold surged through the car and it lurched to the side as Lori threw himself into the passenger seat and banged his boots against the doorframe. He wasn't a big man. Average height and burly like a boxer. Still not so big that he would tilt a car. No, this was all for the drama. Vaughn looked away until she was sure her face was neutral.

"I know you have snow in Spokane, too." She kept her voice flat, aware that she was poking the bear, but also sure that getting him out of the house had been a point in her favor.

Lori slammed the door and stretched his seatbelt across himself. "Inventory on Christmas night? Is that really necessary?"

"Just another Saturday to a lotta people." Vaughn put the car in gear and slowly backed out of the driveway, mindful of the decorations her father had arranged in the yard to welcome Lori home for the holiday.

"Inventory," he snarled. "I should teach you how to liquidate when the place shuts down."

Vaughn tightened her grip on the steering wheel. Every conversation came down to this: Lori talking about closing the bar, her grandfather's business for fifty years, and her livelihood plus that of seven other people. "It's a successful bar."

"Yeah. At what cost?" Lori crossed his arms. "Watch out for black ice. Who buys a house on a fucking hill? Your brilliant mother does."

About to mention that they'd never had to bail out the basement, Vaughn remembered her vow not to fight and let the words fizzle out on her tongue.

Lori tried to start several conversations, but even when he adjusted his tone, everything he said was caustic. Vaughn drove in silence. Eventually, Lori stopped talking. Either he was disappointed he wasn't getting a fight, or he realized he'd lost the ability to converse without being an ass. Vaughn didn't care which was true. She was glad he was finally fucking quiet.

When they arrived, Vaughn parked in the back and then let Lori in the building, directing him to the office. "You want the basement or the bar?" Vaughn took a tablet from the locked cabinet behind the desk.

Lori shrugged out of his coat and hung it on the rack near the door. "Doesn't matter. What's the tablet for?"

"Re-order." Vaughn brought the device to life and walked him through the system, showing him how to request next-day delivery.

"Slick. When'd Dad get this?"

"Two years ago. Saves a lot of money and we hardly ever run out of anything now."

"Nice." Lori looked up from the device and huffed. "Stuff like this will get us a better price when Dad finally sells."

Reminding herself not to engage, Vaughn gave him a tight smile. "Basement or bar?"

"Basement."

She nodded.

"No tablet for you?"

"App's on my phone. iPad is easier for Gramps. He says he doesn't fat finger on it."

Lori tucked the tablet under his arm and clambered down the stairs to inventory the kegs.

She didn't bother to open her app. Instead, she wiped down the gleaming white granite of the bar, then all the tables, setting the chairs on the ground. As she went, she spritzed the evergreen garlands that hung over the bar and around the windows with water, refreshing the scent, and plugged in the twinkle lights twisted around them. She unlocked the door and flicked on the "open" sign. She hadn't made it back behind the counter before she had four occupied stools.

"You're a star for opening early."

"Only fifteen minutes." She set a pint glass on the counter and gestured to the taps.

The man pointed to a local brew. "Fifteen minutes that I wasn't staring at the sign, waiting for the light to come on."

"I only posted about opening thirty minutes ago." Vaughn knew people would come out on Christmas night, but it'd never occurred to her that they'd be waiting at the door.

"And I left my husband fighting with his parents two hours ago. It's too cold to run out my frustration."

"I feel that." Vaughn lined up his glass and moved on to the next patron, noting a tab for the regular she'd just served. She'd pulled several drafts and opened a new bottle of whiskey by the time her uncle burst through the doors from the back.

"You guys are drinking like fish!" He stopped in his tracks. "What're all these people doing here? It's Christmas!"

"If you knew my mother, you'd understand!" someone shouted from the dartboard area.

"And my roommate," a guy in a University of Michigan sweatshirt said.

"My uncle is the fucking devil." A woman threw herself onto a stool. "Can I get a tequila, please?"

Vaughn didn't miss her uncle's blush. She hid her smile as she poured the drink.

"My aunt knitted me a pair of underwear and wanted me to model it," a young woman sitting with the University of Michigan guy shouted.

Vaughn winced. "Gross."

"I hope she at least used nice yarn," the tequila woman said.

Lori coughed over a laugh.

"I proposed in front of my entire family, and she said no!" A guy violently threw a dart, making his fellow players cringe. "Now my mother cries every time she looks at me."

"Your drinks are on me, mate," Lori said. "What's he got?"

"Draft beer." Vaughn hefted up a full tray of drinks. "We can do inventory in the morning. I have to run these out. Make sure everyone's topped off."

5

Lori blinked a few times as Vaughn moved around him. "Specials?"

"Nope."

"Open any tabs?"

"Yep."

"Got it." Lori nodded and worked his way down the bar, making fresh drinks.

For the first time all night, he wasn't picking fights. In fact, Vaughn got a glimpse of the man she'd known as a child: jovial, outgoing, willing to listen to those who needed to talk.

They worked well as a team, trading ends of the bar as people kept coming through the doors.

"We need another case of winter lager," Lori said. "Can you handle everyone up here for a few minutes?"

There was a clatter as Cheyenne came in. "I got her back." The woman shrugged out of her coat, leaving strings of tinsel in her wake, and kissed Vaughn's cheek. "Thank you for getting me out of that damn party."

Vaughn smiled. "Sign in and stow your coat."

Cheyenne pulled her hair into a messy knot. "Should we do a special on peppermint schnapps?" she asked with an impish grin.

"No." An older man at the bar was firm in his answer. "Absolutely not. I came here to escape my mother and mother-in-law arguing. You know what they were drinking? Got damn peppermint schnapps. It's not a holiday drink. It's an amateur drink. I plan to get drunk properly."

Vaughn chuckled and topped off the man's whiskey.

"Vaughn!"

She perked up at the familiar voice. "Dylan!"

Dylan swept through the bar and wrapped Vaughn in a hug before giving her a smacking kiss. "You're doing God's work."

Vaughn rolled her eyes. If her uncle hadn't spent the entire holiday raising her grandfather's blood pressure, she probably would've stayed in. This wasn't charity. It was preserving her sanity and her grandfather's health.

"Truly. I think my family and I may have broken each other, and being able to tell them I had to work was the perfect excuse to get me out of there. Bless you."

Her heart melted for her friend. Dylan was usually unflappably upbeat. "Sign in. Then tell me what happened."

Vaughn replaced beers for the people sitting at the bar. Then she settled in at the washing station, making quick work of the empties that had stacked up while she and Lori had been on their own.

Cheyenne came back with a list of orders from the tables as Dylan tied an apron around their waist and helped her line up the glasses. As the three of them fell into their usual rhythm, Vaughn flicked a little bell that hung near the cash register year-round. It was how her grandfather let the team know he was glad they were there. She rang it as much for him as for herself.

7

CHAPTER TWO

V AUGHN GROWLED AS Lori dumped more glasses into the bar sink, slopping water all over her. Giving him the fight he wanted wasn't worth it. Not when her grandfather would ask how the evening went and see straight through a lie. Disappointing him was worse than a hangover from cheap booze. She finished washing the glasses and attended to the people sitting closest to her.

Gusty, a man who'd been a regular for at least ten years, waved and got her attention as she served people near him. "How's it going with Lori?"

Vaughn turned toward her uncle. He joked with someone as he mixed a drink. "Better now that we're here. He's human with customers."

"Progress. I'm surprised he agreed to work on Christmas."

"He didn't." Vaughn shook her head. "Not like this, anyway. I told him we needed to do inventory and pre-order for New Year's."

"You had the New Year's order in before Thanksgiving."

"He doesn't know that. I turned on the 'open' sign while he was in the basement." She didn't feel bad about tricking Lori. She wanted him away from the family for a few hours, but she also needed to not have to constantly deal with him and his designs to yank her job out from under her. Opening the bar felt like the best way to accomplish both goals.

Gusty guffawed. "That's a little evil."

"And a lot effective." Vaughn resumed her place at the washing station. Lori had filled it in the three minutes she had taken to serve customers. "He flies home on the 27th. I've already picked out the scotch I'm gonna drink to celebrate."

Gusty held out his fist. "You can make it, girl."

Vaughn tapped her knuckles against his. "Keep the bail fund running, just in case. The way he's going, he's gonna give Cil another stroke. And at Cil's age? It could kill him. Then I'll have to kill Lori."

"Your grandfather and this bar are Ann Arbor bedrock. Justice'll be on your side."

"Vaughn." Lori banged his fist against the bar. He dumped more glasses into the sink, slopped more water. If not for the drain mats on the floor, she'd be standing in a puddle.

She ground her teeth, biting back the rebuke she desperately wanted to dish out.

"Why you giving out more darts. You want people here all night?"

"Yeah." She looked him straight in the eye. "Profit."

He knocked on the counter again.

She raised her eyebrows, waiting for him to speak. She'd handed him an opportunity to mention closing the bar–again; would he take it? He needed to come to terms with the fact that Crawford's still had a lot of good years left.

He glared until someone called his name. Another knock, then he walked away.

She closed her eyes to rein in her frustration, then resumed washing.

Gusty whistled and tipped his glass to her before taking a drink. "Maybe you should have a shot of that scotch now."

"It'll taste so much better when he's gone." Vaughn scanned the room, careful to check the beer mirrors on the opposite wall, hung strategically so the bartenders could see every bit of the room. She caught a hand signal from Cheyenne. Vaughn repeated it to confirm. When Cheyenne nodded, Vaughn lined up pint glasses for drafts.

Gusty glanced over his shoulder and snorted. "What on earth is she wearing?"

Vaughn smiled, then laughed when Cheyenne dusted tinsel off a customer. "She came from an ugly sweater contest."

"She win?"

"Nope."

Gusty laughed. "She wears it too well."

A guy with blocky spikes, a rainbow scarf, and a giant steaming tray walked up to the bar. "I'm looking for Vaughn."

"That's me." She lifted her chin as she poured a beer.

"Nice." He smiled. "I was looking for a guy."

Vaughn shrugged. Except for her dad, a self-proclaimed "outlaw," everyone in her family had old-school Irish names: Cillian, Lorcan, Maeve. Hers was only different in that typically men had it. Her mother—Maeve—said when she was born her father had declared no other name suited Vaughn. The remaining options had been Saoirse and Roisin, which would've sentenced her to a lifetime of teaching pronunciation. "Family name. What's up?"

"My aunt called the owner and told him she had extra food. He said to ask for you. I've got a few more trays and serving stuff."

"Wow, thanks!" Vaughn wiped off a spot on the bar. "Put it here. What's your name?"

"Darryl Black. Nice to meet you." He extended his hand over the tray.

"Vaughn Williams." She bumped his knuckles.

Another guy with food lined up next to Darryl. "This is Chris."

"Hey, Chris." Vaughn made room for more trays. "You guys planning to stay awhile?"

"Yeah," Chris said. "We can't start band practice without our guitarist."

"Band?" Gusty leaned over.

Darryl smiled as he unwound his scarf. "Words Fail Me."

"I've heard your stuff on college radio," Gusty said. "Not bad."

"Thanks." Darryl gave a casual salute.

"Tell your friends," Chris said with a smile.

Vaughn chuckled. "Your first round's on me. What'll you have?"

"Imma see if Justin needs help with the rest." Chris spun on his heel and booked it out the door.

"Thanks for the round." Darryl showed her his license. "Chris is only twenty. Can you put whatever you give him in a pilsner, so he doesn't stand out? These last few months are making him nuts."

Vaughn gave him a warm smile. "We keep a healthy stock of sodas in long neck bottles. Or I can do the pilsner thing."

Darryl returned her smile. "He likes ginger ale."

"Done. And for you?"

"Whatever's on draft."

"I've got eight beers on draft and a decent selection in bottles." She slid a paper menu to him. "Take your pick. Like I said, on me. Don't worry about the price."

"Thanks." Darryl scanned the menu.

"Hey." A guy with long, honey-blond hair and an olive-green coat nudged Darryl and set down two more huge trays, and rested a big, solid-looking hand on them, as though making sure they were safely placed on the counter. "Last ones. Chris is getting the serving stuff."

Vaughn took a step back. The tenor of his voice ran straight down her spine and raised the hairs on the back of her neck. She blinked a few times to regain her

13

sense. Who was this man and how did he manage to stun her before she even made eye contact?

"What's all this?" Dylan asked as they returned from the game area. They loaded dirty glasses into the sink and started washing.

"The owner here did my aunt a solid a while back," Darryl said. "She had a catering job cancel at the last minute. Most of it went to Food Gathers, but they couldn't take everything. She saw the post about you guys opening and figured people needed snacks to balance their drinking."

"She's awesome," Dylan said. "What'd she send?"

"Bao, pork, shrimp shumai." Darryl tapped the trays as he announced the food. "And Justin brought in the sweet corn fritters."

"Bao?" Cheyenne sailed behind the bar, tinsel still dripping from her sweater, and dumped empty bottles into the recycle bin. "With the magic pork?"

Darryl laughed. "I don't know if it's magic, but yeah, the bao has pork in it."

"If it's from Lee's, it's magic," Cheyenne said.

"I'll have to tell Auntie you said that."

"Please do." Cheyenne leaned her elbows on the bar and let loose a flirty smile. "And let me buy you a drink."

Vaughn didn't roll her eyes, though she wanted to. Cheyenne hated being hit on at work—which was common, given her model looks—but she was the first to flirt when she saw someone she liked. "I already got their first round, Chey."

Cheyenne laughed and lifted the tray Vaughn had prepared. "Then I got the second. I bet you guys'll drink free all night." She sailed back to her tables.

"What are you having?" Vaughn asked.

Darryl scrunched his face. "This is a big ask, but could we get two Kentucky Breakfast Stouts?"

"Absolutely." Vaughn gave him a wide smile. "That's an excellent choice. The bourbon flavor in it... mmm."

"You like bourbon?" Darryl's friend asked.

Vaughn turned her gaze to him, and froze for a moment, staring into eyes so blue they reminded her of the summer sky. "I like all the whiskeys."

He smiled and leaned against the bar. "Same."

Vaughn gave him a long look, her gaze resting on his hand, now in a loose fist on the bar. She backed away, realizing she was leering.

Gusty snickered and gulped the rest of his Natty Lite.

This time, Vaughn did roll her eyes. "I got it. And if Gusty goes back to his best behavior, I'll pull him a fresh beer too."

She popped the caps off two bottles of the requested stout and handed them over before digging out a bottle of ginger ale.

Chris returned with serving supplies as Vaughn made a few quick decisions about where to put the trays.

"Hey!" Lori called. "This ain't no hipster brewery with food trucks outside." He stomped over. "You guys ordered takeout at fucking work?"

15

Vaughn finished arranging plates and utensils before she responded. "A local business donated it."

"Actually, the best Chinese place in the city," Dylan said.

"What a Christmas miracle," Lori sneered.

Darryl's friend bristled, adding guilt to Vaughn's frustration.

"We have this handled." Vaughn glowered at Lori, willing the man to back down.

"Sure. Sure." Lori took a plate and heaped food onto it.

Vaughn and Dylan exchanged incredulous looks. Lori had been raised in this bar, just as Vaughn had, and knew Cil would blow his top if he saw Lori disrespecting another local business. Cil required better.

With a plate full of food and one eye on a woman a few seats away, Lori said, "You guys gonna sling drinks or what?"

"Whaddya think I've been doing?" Cheyenne's empty tray clattered on the bar. She made a face at Lori as she filled it with bottles of beer and headed back toward the tables. Dylan followed with food and serving supplies.

"D." Chris knocked against his friend's shoulder. "Doesn't she look like the chick from that video?"

"Who?"

"The chick with the fuzzy sweater. She's over there with the dude in the skirt."

"You mean Cheyenne," Gusty said. "The dude is Dylan. But don't call them a dude."

Chris nodded at Gusty. "Thanks for the tip. And yeah. Cheyenne. D, who's the girl from the hair band video we watched yesterday? She was all over the Jags."

"Seriously?" the third guy asked. "You have to do this here?"

Chris shrugged, though he seemed a little contrite. "We all see her."

"Shut it, man," Darryl said.

Gusty chuckled. "Cheyenne does take after Tawny Kitaen in the Whitesnake video."

Chris snapped his fingers. "Yes! Thank you!"

"Some advice." Vaughn set a bottle of ginger ale in front of Chris. "Don't mention that to her."

"She must get that a lot," the hot guy said.

Vaughn nodded. "From men old enough to be her father."

Gusty clinked his glass against the counter. "And then some."

"Awkward." Chris took a long pull off the ginger ale and then studied the bottle.

"And naturally you're the one to bring it up, asshole." Darryl pushed Chris a few steps away from the bar.

They still stood close enough that it worried Vaughn. "Hey." She leaned across the counter and gestured for the third guy to come closer. She hoped what she was about to say wouldn't disappoint. "Are you Justin?"

"Yeah. Nice to meet you." He flashed one of his hands, revealing calluses on his palms, and gave her a smile that had her wishing her hair wasn't in a haphazard ponytail and her clothes weren't spattered with dishwater.

She put her ego behind her and focused on business. "I'm Vaughn. Not trying to be a buzzkill, but I can't let Chris sit at the bar."

"No problem. We'll get a table."

She nodded to one across the room. "If you guys take that one, I'll be able to see when you're ready for refills." Mostly, she wanted to see Justin. Thankfully, his underage friend and all the food they'd brought gave her a valid excuse to keep an eye on them.

He smiled. "Appreciate it, but we can cover our tab."

"Most of these folks had a rough day. They'll be grateful for the food. And Cil would fire me for taking your money."

He dipped his head. "Thank you."

"You guys have a sign for the restaurant?"

"I don't know." Justin turned sideways. "Hey, D, did your aunt give you a sign?"

"Hell no. That's not what this is for."

Vaughn shook her head. "That's not how we roll."

"I got it, boss." Dylan rifled around the cash register and turned up several small dry erase boards.

"Boss?" Lori puffed out his chest and spoke around the food in his mouth. "That's a bit of a stretch."

Of course, Lori had ignored them—and the minor at the bar—until he saw an opportunity for a fight.

"*You're* a bit of a stretch," Dylan said.

Vaughn squeezed their shoulder, hoping to telegraph a message not to argue. It didn't matter that Lori hadn't been officially on staff at Crawford's in five years. Lori had always considered himself above everyone but Cil. Based on his current warpath to close the bar, he might've given himself a promotion.

"She works side-by-side with Cil every day." Dylan uncapped a marker and leaned over one of the boards. "Now shut it and eat your free bao."

Lori glared but plopped another bao on his plate before turning his back on them again.

"Come on, fellas," Justin said. "The lady pointed out a table for us." He led his friends to the area Vaughn had suggested.

She held her gaze steady on his retreating figure, cataloging his broad shoulders, and how his hair swept just past them. And his jeans. They weren't skinny jeans, but they hugged his thighs in an almost indecent way.

"Vaughn Williams, that's quite a Christmas present." Gusty's words snapped her to attention.

Vaughn blinked to recalibrate. "Right? I wasn't expecting catering." A swell of pride rose in her. Cil's generosity to the community was at the core of his personality. It never failed to amaze him when his generosity was returned. He considered himself a small fish in a big pond, but in many ways, the pond wouldn't be so large and thriving if not for him. It was one more reason Vaughn bristled every time Lori mentioned closing the bar. No one would benefit, even if it did net Cil a big pile of money for retirement.

"I meant the guy. He intrigues you."

"Everyone's intriguing until they've got a beer or two in them." One of the biggest occupational hazards Vaughn faced was seeing too many charismatic people turn into creeps after a few drinks.

Gusty feigned dismay. "Are you saying you don't find me charming anymore?"

Vaughn laughed. "You're the exception that proves the rule." She snuck a glance at Justin, only to catch him watching her. Her cheeks burned when he smiled. She turned her attention to wiping down the granite. When there was a lull, she'd go brush her hair. It was a dingy shade between blonde and brown, but she could make it shine. She had a clean shirt in the basement too, one that didn't reek of dishwater. Then she'd add a few extra bottles to her refill order for the beer he was drinking and invite Justin to come back on a quiet night.

CHAPTER THREE

VAUGHN DIDN'T GET to change her sweater during the next two hours, though she did put on a bib apron. Lori seemed to make it his mission to get sink water and drink remnants on her at every opportunity. She mostly overlooked it as a steady stream of customers kept her busy, and her uncle safe from anything worse than an evil eye from her as they worked. She emerged from changing a keg in the basement to find her senior bartenders game planning.

"Should we open the back room?" Dylan asked.

"We'll at least need a barback if we do that." Cheyenne pulled a long piece of tinsel from her sweater and draped it on Dylan's head like a crown. "We can't manage both rooms with only the three of us."

Cheyenne didn't include Lori in her staff tally.

"People seem patient tonight," Vaughn said. Crawford's had been around long enough to be considered an institution, which meant the locals knew they'd be taken care of. Plus, based on some of the holiday stories they'd heard tonight, most people seemed to want a place to be that wasn't where they'd come from. Drinking happened to be an extra perk.

"Someone's gonna wanna work." Dylan ran a hand through their hair and transferred the tinsel to Vaughn's ponytail.

"Even with Lori here?" Vaughn asked.

"Hell yes. We can ignore him. If their days were anything like mine..." Dylan waved the words away. "Put out a group text. Make it voluntary. I'll give them my tips."

Cheyenne gasped.

Vaughn plucked more tinsel from Cheyenne's sleeve and decorated Dylan again. "You earn *good* tips, Dyl."

"Being here is the best tip tonight. I don't need any more fire eyes from my family."

"Fire eyes?" Vaughn asked. "What happened?"

Dylan smoothed the pleats at the waist of their floor-length skirt. "Nothing terrible. I just needed a break." They gestured toward the room. "I'm not the only one."

"I'll send a group text." Cheyenne fished her phone out of her apron pocket.

"Volunteers only." Vaughn didn't want anyone to feel obligated to work. But if more staffers needed a change of scenery, she'd happily pay them and encourage generous tips.

She scanned the room and nodded to Justin. She pulled two new bottles of the stout he and Darryl were drinking from the cooler, along with another ginger ale.

He rounded the table and walked toward her, an easy smile on his chiseled face. He leaned against the counter when he got there, opened his wallet, and thumbed through bills.

"Nope. This one's on Dylan."

Justin lifted an eyebrow. "You sure? They didn't volunteer."

"They told me they were next."

"You guys are something else. Lemme leave a tip."

Vaughn shook her head both to decline the tip and mentally reset. Why couldn't she stop staring at this man? "When my staff covers your tab, no tips. We have our reasons."

Justin smiled again.

Attractive people flirting with bartenders were a dime a dozen. His tab would've been covered anyway because of the metric ton of food he and his friends had brought in. But that smile... if Vaughn didn't know Gusty would tease her about it, she'd put on lipstick as soon as Justin walked away, then get his attention and kiss him, making sure enough lipstick stayed on him that he thought of her next time he looked in a mirror.

He must've known what she was thinking because he looked at her lips, then back at her eyes. "Thank you."

She couldn't let him walk away yet, so she used the first thing she could find to keep him talking. "Mechanical engineer?" She she rose on her toes to see all the symbols and their captions on his T-shirt. Multi-tasking, beer, sarcasm, adult language. "What does it say in the corner?"

Justin pulled out the shirt. "Ah, she changed it. I don't know what the caption said before, but Renee changed it to 'long hours may cause binge drumming.' I'm also a drummer." He tapped a rhythm on the bar that sounded vaguely like Whitesnake.

"Renee?" Spending most of her formative years around the bar had given Vaughn a top-notch poker face. Justin wouldn't see her dread at the idea of him having a girlfriend.

"Yeah. Darryl's sister. Her girlfriend knitted rainbow scarves for everyone, and Renee made us semi-custom shirts."

Fantasy preserved, at least for now, Vaughn kept the conversation going. "Why semi-custom?"

"She's in a pretty rigorous post-grad program. She likes personal gifts but lacks time."

"Do you?"

"Lack time? Nah." He pointed to the square on his shirt. "Multi-tasker."

Vaughn smiled. "Same."

"Just!" Chris called out.

Justin glanced over his shoulder as Chris made a throwing gesture.

"Oh, yeah." Justin faced her again. "Is it okay if the guys open the last dartboard?"

"Sure." Vaughn took out a small box of darts and passed it to him. "We usually have live music on weekends, so we mostly use them during the week. Thinner crowds."

"Fewer people during the week? I'll definitely be back then, so I can talk to you and not feel like I'm monopolizing your time."

Vaughn couldn't break his gaze, even though more people crowded the bar. "You're not monopolizing me."

"Maybe I want to."

Vaughn leaned toward him but lost her train of thought as Lori elbowed his way toward the cooler that held the seasonal beers. "Oof." She adjusted her stance and threw an elbow of her own as Lori passed behind her again.

Justin chuckled and held up the box of darts. "When our singer gets here, we'll play a few songs for you."

"That'd be great." It was a shame he'd be sitting behind the band; though if he was front and center, she'd definitely get herself in trouble for staring.

"Trading music for drinks is better than freebies." Justin collected the fresh drinks and went back to his table.

"Damn, that was smooth." She watched his retreat again, wondering how long it would take him to finish that beer and give her another excuse to talk with him.

"You sure that man isn't your stocking stuffer this year?" Gusty asked.

"Why you talking to my niece like that, Gusty?" Vaughn had no idea where Lori had come from, but he leaned on the bar in front of Gusty, face scrunched as though he'd drunk bad tequila. "I need to cut you off?"

"Give it a rest, Uncle Lori. This is Gusty's version of meddling." Her uncle had been giving her shit since his plane had touched down two days ago, but *now* he wanted to play white knight? Not only was it too little, too late, but if Lori had paid attention to anything other than his own bluster, he would've gotten a better understanding of the dynamics at Crawford's.

Gusty held up a hand. "Lori has a point. Joshin' between friends is one thing." Gusty gave Lori a pointed look. "And Vaughn and I *are* friends." He turned his attention back to Vaughn. "But your uncle isn't out of line. I shouldn't be saying stuff like that with strangers around. They might think harassing you and Cheyenne is okay, and it definitely is *not*."

Vaughn hadn't expected Gusty to fight with Lori, but the way he came to her defense stunned her. Gusty rarely showed humility to men like Lori. Hell, he hardly ever interacted with men like Lori. Gusty was almost fifteen years her senior, and as good a friend to her as anyone she spent time with.

He tapped a finger to his ball cap. "I apologize. I'll watch myself, Lori. You don't need to."

"Thank you." Lori nudged Vaughn. "See? No one mistreats my girls."

Justin took the newly vacated stool next to Gusty. "I thought kids aren't allowed at the bar."

"They aren't," Lori said.

"Then what girls are you talking about? I only see women here."

Gusty buried his face in his shoulder and coughed loudly.

Her poker face pushed past its limit, Vaughn pressed her hand against her mouth to hide her smile.

Lori blinked at Justin. "She's my niece." He stared at Justin for a few seconds. "She'll always be a girl to me."

"But she's an adult, right?" Justin wore an expression of angelic innocence.

"She is," Gusty said. "And we want her treated with the respect adults deserve."

Lori's cheeks pinked. "You two need to watch yourselves." He knocked on the counter, acted like someone needed his attention, and left them.

Vaughn gave a small laugh. "He's been spoiling for a fight, and he just walked away. Gusty, I'm clearing your tab."

"Don't you dare. I took a lotta pleasure in that."

Vaughn riffled through a box by the cash register and slid a pack of Raisinets, his favorite treat, across the counter to Gusty. The man's eyes lit up, and he winked at her as he tore open the box.

"Another stout?" she asked Justin.

"Water, thanks." He gave her a warm smile and pushed the empty bottles from his table toward her.

She traded Justin's bottles for a glass of ice water, replaying his comments that had finally driven Lori away. Her cheeks tingled, and she met Justin's gaze for a moment. "Thanks."

"Okay." Dylan returned and set to washing glasses. "We have to keep an eye on Chey. That not engaged guy is talking to her way more than necessary. She tried to make him feel better about himself and he latched on."

Cheyenne stood midway between the tables and the bar, her tray full of empty glasses. A guy wearing a preppy button-down under a puffy vest seemed on the verge of tears. Cheyenne patted his arm a few times.

"Lori's covering his tab but told him he has to tip. Maybe he'll be generous," Vaughn said.

"It'd be a shame if someone who so closely resembles Thor leaves a shitty gratuity," Dylan said.

"Preach," Vaughn said.

Cheyenne sailed behind the bar. "Lori, I need you to handle I-can't-even-return-the-ring-guy the rest of the night."

Lori laughed. "No harm in flirtin', Chey."

"Seriously?" Vaughn glared at Lori. He'd blustered at Gusty about flirting, and now he was on the verge of pimping out Cheyenne. Vaughn moved toward him, but Cheyenne cut her off.

"He doesn't have enough tattoos for my taste." Cheyenne stashed her tray and entered orders into their register. "And my day was weird enough without being some sad sack's rebound bang."

"Fair," Vaughn said. "Lori, cover the dartboards."

"I got a system going here!" Lori gestured to the area he worked in, the group of guys who Vaughn was certain he knew from high school, sitting across from him. "Besides, if Chey can't handle bar folks, she shouldn't work in one."

Vaughn put a hand on her hip. "I should..." She hesitated. She wanted to tell Lori to fuck off so badly the words seared her tongue. She gave him a flat smile instead. "Chey volunteered tonight. She can leave whenever she wants."

Lori faced Vaughn and knocked on the bar.

Vaughn flashed her eyebrows, mentally daring him to show his ass again. "Or you can help her."

"Well, Lori?" Dylan asked.

Lori flung his hands out. "I entered these tabs by actual name. I don't play around with shit like 'guy in Michigan sweatshirt.' There's one of those every five feet." He slapped the bar.

Dylan turned to Vaughn and rolled his eyes. "Whatever, Lori. I know what everyone's drinking out there."

Lori immediately turned back to the group he'd been talking with.

"Dyl," Cheyenne rested her hand on the back of Dylan's shoulder. "The prairie skirt you're wearing is too good to risk getting dirty. You're safer back here."

"The prairie skirt is meant to be seen."

"Is it designer?" Justin asked.

Gusty nudged Justin with his arm. "Probably. Dylan's bestie works at the Saks in Troy and helps them track down all kinds of avant-garde items."

"Thank you, Gusty." Dylan beamed. "This is a JW Anderson pleated skirt with a custom fit leather belt. I have literally been waiting years for this skirt. It was absolutely worth the drive and vacation time to get it."

"It's beautiful," Vaughn said. "The fabric looks like a good weight, too. Not heavy but enough to keep you warm outside."

"Yes! You people get me. You really do."

Justin leaned forward on the bar. "I have one more question."

"Shoot." Dylan smiled and refreshed Justin's water.

Vaughn paid close attention. Justin had been kind and fun to talk with all night, but if this was the moment when he changed, and asked something off-color, she wouldn't hesitate to kick him out on his very nice ass.

"Are the tailors at Saks good? Darryl's sister said their precision is unmatched."

"Darryl's sister is absolutely correct." Dylan took a step back and flicked their skirt. "Look at this fit. Flawless."

Justin nodded. "Truth."

Dylan beamed. "I'll check on failed engagement guy."

Cheyenne eyed Justin before nodding at another patron and filling a pilsner. "Lori!"

He looked over his shoulder.

"This one's okay." Cheyenne pointed to Justin. "Don't give him any shit."

Lori gave a thumbs up and turned back to his customers.

Vaughn shook her head and winked at Justin. He could stay as long as he wanted.

CHAPTER FOUR

VAUGHN FOLLOWED DYLAN with a tray laden with beers, plus an extra that she dropped on an empty stool. Whether people bussed their own tables, or she and Dylan did, the tray would fill sooner rather than later.

Cil had opened Crawford's intending to be more than a dive, or a hole-in-the-wall. They didn't have a kitchen, but they had an enormous space full of tables, plus a smaller room in the back. Despite the large room, tonight most people sat at the bar, or in the far corner, where tables surrounded three dartboards. As a teenager, Vaughn had asked why they didn't have a pool table, like so many other bars.

"All it takes is one pool cue poking the wrong ass and a fight'll break out. I can't serve drinks and drop kick losers at the same time. Might spill."

Vaughn suspected Cil's colorful answer was only partly true. The rest of the reason was probably that pool tables used more space than drinking tables, and drinking tables made more money.

In the eighties, Cil had succumbed to pressure and added video games. After a few years, the maintenance had become a burden and Cil removed them. Business stayed steady and that area became a flex space. At the moment, a buffet of the food Darryl and his friends had brought occupied it. On Fridays and some Saturdays, it served as a small stage for live music. It was only two steps above the rest of the room, but it got the job done.

Still, Vaughn longed for a real stage. Then she'd have more options for events. Cil had mixed feelings about it, but Vaughn sensed him coming around, especially since he only worked three days a week and no later than eight.

Over the summer, the air conditioning had broken in a nearby bookstore. Rain had been in the forecast, so Vaughn had invited the book club meeting on the sidewalk to reconvene in the cool air at Crawford's. Always supportive of his fellow business owners, Cil hadn't batted an eye when Vaughn turned up with ten women. He'd poured drinks and listened to them discuss books. Vaughn had figured he'd give her grief later, but they'd sold a ton of wine, and Cil had made

DRUMMER BOY FOR CHRISTMAS

a new lady friend. The book club got an open invitation to meet at Crawford's whenever they wanted. Cil even posted their flyer in the hallway leading to the bathrooms. It stood out among the plaques from local team sponsorships and framed newspaper articles about the bar.

Vaughn wiped down a vacated table as Dylan served drinks.

"Thanks for letting us open this board." Darryl sat at a small table, watching Chris and Justin play darts. A long piece of tinsel was woven through his blocky spikes. Had Cheyenne marked him for her own amusement or to subtly tell not-engaged-guy she wasn't interested? Either way, the night could end exceptionally well for him.

"It's my pleasure," Vaughn said. Brash laughter nearby caught her attention.

"You're right, buddy. Not errryone can pull off tha skirt." A man wearing a beanie, a blinking necklace of Christmas lights, and an ill-fitting, red sweater snorted and slurped his beer. "Why not a kilt? Then you get a little fanny pack."

Dylan shook their head. "I wear what I want."

"You don't get groped from behind?" another guy asked.

Vaughn glared and slipped between the tables to intervene and kick the guys out. Even Lori wasn't obnoxious like this.

"Grabbing people is an easy way to get beat up, shit for brains," Chris shouted as he threw his dart. "Just agree they have a nice ass and shut the fuck up."

Vaughn stopped in her tracks and nodded at Dylan as one side of their mouth quirked up.

"But who do you take home at the end of the nighh?" beanie guy asked. "Do you look for chicks with clothes you wanna try on?"

"And you're out." Vaughn rustled in the pockets of her apron for the portable payment terminal.

"You're trowin' me out?" The man looked indignant, despite the spittle on his chin that accumulated with every "t" sound he made.

"Yep." Her credit card machine was dead, but it didn't matter. She snapped a photo of the guy with her phone and then angled around him to get photos of his friends. One of them shook mistletoe attached to his belt at her. She feigned a gag.

"Some chick issa gonna trow me out." He stood and knocked his hat askew, crossing his arms as he teetered.

"The *woman* you're talking to is the reason this bar is open tonight." Dylan produced the receipt for the men's drinks. "You can square up with me before you go."

"You want me to pay before you trow me out?"

"Sure do," Vaughn said.

The man made a show of patting his pockets. "Uh oh. No wallet. Fellas?"

The crew with him all mumbled, none of them opening a wallet or offering money.

Vaughn leaned toward Dylan. "Go tell Lori he needs to remove these guys."

"Yeah, no. I'm not ceding space to these assholes."

"Dylan."

"I'm not leaving you alone with them. They outnumber you in both bodies and stupidity."

Vaughn took a deep breath. "Don't make me laugh right now." Dylan preferred laughter to angst, and Vaughn usually didn't mind following suit. Too many people cried in bars.

"They're right." Justin flanked her other side. "These guys are trouble. I can get them to leave."

"Thanks, but I got this." "I know." Justin angled his body between her and beanie guy, who yelled about how ballsy it was that he had to pay his bill. "I can help. I'll get Lori."

Beanie guy pushed Justin. "I need to talk to the beer wench."

"Now you're annoying the shit out of me!" Chris stomped up to the table and grabbed beanie guy's coat, and the coat from the chair next to it. "You assholes need to go." He stomped toward the door and threw the coats outside.

"Shit," Vaughn whispered. Dealing with a belligerent drunk was one thing; someone else getting into the mix made everything more complicated.

"Fuckin' Chris," Justin muttered. "You!" He raised his voice and strode toward beanie guy, who was trying unsuccessfully to intimidate Chris. "It's time to go."

"Maybe my wallet was in tha coat!"

"Yeah. You should check." Justin adjusted his posture and seemed to expand and fill twice the space. He didn't touch the guy, but he used his body to force the man to the exit. Once he got beanie guy outside, Justin closed the door behind him and cast a glare at the man's friends.

"Well, I guess that's settled." Vaughn gave Dylan a tight smile, threaded her arm through theirs, and walked to the bar.

"You're just gonna let hottie engineer man and his foodie friends deal with that?"

"It's that or climb him like a tree." Watching Justin toss that drunk asshole out without laying a finger on him, let alone barely raising his voice, had been a glorious dose of competence porn.

"Ooh!" Dylan stretched out the word as they whispered in a high pitch.

Vaughn laughed. "Let's send Lori to make sure the guy's friends leave."

Dylan squeezed Vaughn's arm before they separated to slip back behind the bar.

"Uncle Lori, these guys—" Vaughn showed him the photos on her phone "—need to leave. If they need a ride, Crawford's will pay for it."

"You want them gone so bad you'll pay?" Lori waved toward the group, who were now complaining loudly about being forced to leave.

"Yep."

"You wanna kick 'em out on Christmas. Knowing they're all sad sacks?" Lori gave her a long look, but Vaughn didn't flinch. "You got it." He put down the rag that hung over his shoulder and pushed up his sleeves as he made his way to the darts area, where the annoying guys were taking forever to put on their coats.

"That was too easy," Dylan said.

Vaughn nodded as she shifted her attention to the people at the counter. She hadn't finished making the next drink when Lori's voice broke through the din.

"You slow ass mother fuckers make grannies seem fast! Let's go!" He clapped, then put his hands on his hips. "Eh. I don't mind tossing you out." Lori grabbed one of the men by the back of the collar and dragged him toward the door.

Dylan sighed.

"Yeah. Shoulda seen that coming," Vaughn said.

CHAPTER FIVE

A FLICKER OF MOVEMENT in the mirror caught Vaughn's eye as Justin worked his way through the growing crowd. He moved with ease between each group, angling his shoulders as he approached the bar. By the time she'd finished making a round of drinks, he stood next to Gusty. "I hope I didn't overstep. Chris pushes the envelope sometimes."

Vaughn shrugged. "Not how I would've done it, but creativity helps with persistent drunks."

"Well, Chris gets the points for creativity."

Vaughn blanched.

"Don't worry, we don't encourage him."

Cheyenne hung an arm around Vaughn and sipped a beer. "You should make this your regular bar."

Justin grinned. "Thanks."

Loud laughter from the dartboards broke through the din. Chris and Lori play wrestled each other for throws. Darryl looked at Vaughn, shrugged, and took a pull of his beer.

"See?" Justin said. "They're goofing around, or Darryl would reel Chris in."

Chris won the dart, and Lori straightened, gripping his lower back.

"Looks like Lori might need to be reeled in," Gusty said.

"Seriously." Cheyenne tossed a bottle in the recycle bin. "Not only does he think he's still twenty-five, he's also trying to show off."

Vaughn pulled a draft. "Give him a few more minutes. He'll tweak something pretty good and come back."

Darryl nudged in next to Justin. "Can I get water?"

Cheyenne reached across the counter and tapped one of Darryl's spikes, then his chin. "Sure."

He angled his head toward her. "Thinking about breaking out the flat iron and going full-scale emo hair."

"No, thank you." Cheyenne handed him a cup of icy water.

"Some dude trying to cover his bald spot came up with that style." Justin knocked his shoulder against Darryl. "And we're not an emo band. No false advertising."

Vaughn laughed. "Wise."

Two men whom Vaughn recognized as Lori's friends stood and put on their jackets. She printed their bills and dropped them in front of them, each tucked into a check holder. "Thanks, guys."

One man squinted at her and the other glanced at the checks as he reached into his back pocket. "Uh. Yeah. Thanks."

Vaughn stepped away and washed a few glasses, giving the men space to pay.

"We're all set!" The squinty man called out. He waved as he walked away.

"Thanks!" Vaughn collected their trays and looked up as the door closed behind them. Both receipts were jammed together with five dollars. Convinced that Lori's friends wouldn't skip out, she skirted around the counter to see if a few bills or maybe a credit card had fallen on the floor. Nothing. She clenched her jaw as she strode to the exit and stepped into the glacial night. The men were long gone, and she didn't blame them. They'd stolen from her. And it was fucking cold. She ducked back inside, rubbing her arms.

"Everything okay, Vaughn?" Dylan asked.

She grunted as she returned to the bar, where Cheyenne worked alone. Lori still hung around the dartboards and continued fake wrestling. "Cheyenne, are these tabs accurate?"

Cheyenne reviewed each slip and handed them back. "As far as I can tell."

Vaughn held up the wrinkled five-dollar bill.

Dylan fumbled a glass. "That's all they left?"

Vaughn nodded.

"That's not even a buck a drink between them," Cheyenne said.

"I know." Vaughn stowed the receipt plates, blood pounding in her temples over being stiffed. On Christmas. When everyone working had volunteered. She faced the room and let loose a field whistle, probably the only useful thing her uncle had taught her.

The entire bar stilled. Lori turned and stared at her like he'd been trapped in a police spot light. She waved him in.

He crossed toward her as the sound picked up again. "What's wrong?"

She gave him the receipts and the money. "This is what your buddies paid on a ninety-dollar tab."

"Shit." Lori shoved the receipts in his pocket and the cash in the tip jar. "I'll take care of it."

Vaughn cocked her head. Why was he calm now? It made no sense and amped her aggravation with him. "I tried to catch them, but they're gone."

"What?" Lori's face flushed. "What the fuck, Vaughn. You don't chase people into the night and you sure as shit don't do it to my friends."

"Which has you angrier?" The throbbing in her temples intensified. "You worried I might embarrass some thieves? On Christmas?"

"Really, Vaughn?"

"Really!" She looked to the ceiling, working to reign in her temper. She lowered her voice when she spoke next. "You keep talking about closing this place like it's floundering. It isn't. And even if it was, that's not an excuse to let your duster friends shit on us."

Lori got in her space. "I said I'd handle it," he growled.

"Call them." She refused to be intimidated.

"Vaughn."

"Lori." They stared at each other for a moment before Vaughn relented. Crawford's was busy. "Handle it."

"Fine." Lori stepped away.

Dylan met Vaughn's gaze as he lifted a newly filled tray. "You alright?"

Vaughn rolled her shoulders. "Annoyed his friends stiffed us."

"It's a misunderstanding. Lori'll make up the difference and get the cash from his guys later."

She lifted another tray, prepared to follow Dylan. "You're awfully optimistic for a seasoned bartender."

Dylan laughed. "'Tis the season. Goodwill toward men and all that shit."

When Vaughn returned to the bar, Cheyenne worked on her own, handling customers lined up three deep. Lori was there, but he'd parked his ass by his friends who hadn't left yet and ignored everyone else. Vaughn immediately got to work, only pausing long enough to notice Gusty's wife had arrived, and give her a proper greeting.

"LORCAN HAYES YOU NEVER CALL ME." A petite woman with big hair and a giant puffy coat stalked through the room.

45

Lori straightened as though he'd taken a bolt of electricity to the spine. He dashed around the counter and stopped her short. "Hey, Sheryl."

"When were you gonna tell me you were in town?" She stomped a stiletto.

"Is he, is he blushing?" Cheyenne asked.

Vaughn snickered. "Oh, this is too good. I wish Cil was here."

"Is that the one-night stand who wouldn't go away?" Dylan asked.

"You mean the woman he strung along for two years before he moved to Spokane? Yes." Memories of Sheryl coming in distraught for weeks after Lori's move came back to Vaughn in a flash. Her turning up now was a sweet dose of karma. Between how Lori had treated her and the bitching he'd been doing all week, the man was due some grief.

"Everyone watch. Watch." Dylan clapped their hands. "This is going to be brilliant."

Justin raised his eyebrows.

"Truly," Vaughn said. "Lori has this coming. Please enjoy it."

"Is his name really Lorcan?" Justin asked.

"Yep. Like Lycan. But he's too... *him* to be a were-wolf, so..." Vaughn waved in Lori's direction, as if that explained it.

"Unkind words about your uncle?" Gusty asked with a broad grin.

"Don't get me started. Lichen in a forest is infinitely more useful than he's been this week."

Gusty snickered.

"Speaking of getting started." Cheyenne nodded toward Lori and his guest.

Sheryl ripped her hat off and threw it at Lori's chest as she scolded him for not answering her calls and texts.

Lori held his hands up. "Honey, let's go in the back."

"No!" Her response was loud and shrill. "No more hiding me, Lori!"

He turned a dark shade of red as he glanced around the room, clearly at a loss.

"This is much more interesting than the drama my mother started at dinner." Gusty's wife said. She tapped her glass against his.

Sheryl stripped off her coat and flung it around him, using the sleeves to drag him toward her. He must've been in shock because the tiny woman got him into a chair.

She pushed down his shoulders. "You have to own your dickishness right here, in your father's bar, in front of God and everyone." She looked around the room. "Where's Cil?"

"Home!" Cheyenne shouted.

"Taking a break from Lori," Vaughn said.

Lori had the grace to look sheepish.

"I know he needed it!" Sheryl sat on Lori's lap and tore into him. She kept her voice low, but bits and pieces of her rant rose above the din. Things like "time zone" and "long-distance charges don't exist."

Gusty chuckled. "Looks like he's gonna be at least as excited as you are for that flight home, Vaughn."

"You're leaving?" Justin asked.

Vaughn focused her attention on him, certain she'd heard disappointment in his voice. "Not me. Lori. I'm staying right here."

"Excellent." Justin's eyes sparkled as he smiled.

She returned his smile but kept it casual. Vaughn had no doubt there was more behind the question, but she wasn't ready to consider more than flirting. He was new, and she had to focus on keeping Lori from driving Cil to his grave.

Cheyenne pressed her lips together, then clicked her tongue. "Vaughn, now that Lori's tied up, I'm down a man to get beer from the basement."

Vaughn surveyed the room. "Nah. We're supposed to be closed tonight. People can wait a few minutes. What needs to come up?"

Cheyenne listed several beers.

"And keg four is mostly foam," Dylan said. "I'll go with you. It'll be faster."

A new round of people flooded the bar. "No, stay here, get your tips. I'll be quick."

"We can help," Justin said, pointing to Darryl.

"I shouldn't let you back here, but thank you."

"We're both of age and we won't sue you if we fall on the stairs," Darryl said, hand against his heart.

Vaughn relented, knowing they would save her time. "I'll line up the cases. You guys bring them to the door. No serving."

Justin hopped off his stool. "You're the boss."

Vaughn cleared people away and opened the pass to let Darryl and Justin back. She left them at the basement door as she turned on the lights and went downstairs. "Wait right there."

"I swear, I'll hold the banister," Darryl shouted behind her.

Vaughn laughed. "Stay put. Last time I was down here, I lined things up that were low. The first case will come your way in a second." She loaded two boxes of beer onto the pulley system she and her grandfather had made together and sent them up.

"Cool!" Darryl swung the two-by-two platform toward himself and unloaded the beer. "How much more?"

"A few boxes," Vaughn called back.

"Nice pulley setup," Justin said. "Is it custom?"

Vaughn laughed. "In a manner of speaking."

"Coming back to you," he said. "Nice rope. Takes the weight well. Easy to grip."

"That was the idea." Vaughn adjusted the platform, added boxes, and then pulled on the rope to send it up. "Cil had a stroke fifteen years ago. He still has some weakness in his left hand. It was important to have something sturdy that he could use with either hand."

"He chose well."

A tug on the ropes indicated that one of the guys had taken over, so she let go. "Thanks. I need to reload once more." She pulled out two bottles of rum and set them next to the last case of beer she intended to send up.

"Okay, going down," Darryl said. "Did you make this system?"

Vaughn hesitated, worried her deep ties to Crawford's would end Justin's flirting. Then she remembered Sheryl shouting about Lori coming clean in his father's bar. Vaughn's connection was clear. "Yeah. It was my eighth-grade science fair project. The rope is ten years old."

"Justin," Darryl said.

"I know." He groaned.

"Know what? If I somehow built a simple pulley incorrectly, it doesn't matter. Thing's been working great all this time." She pulled on the rope. "Last one."

"You made it perfectly," Justin said.

"Thanks. Take those boxes to the front. I'll switch out the keg, then come up."

"Sounds good," Darryl said. "We'll unload and send it back."

"Perfect. Thanks!" Vaughn changed out the empty keg and decided to put a spare in the reserve position. She didn't think they'd need it, but she also hadn't thought she'd be changing kegs tonight at all, let alone twice. She carried the spent keg to the walk-in.

She tugged on the handle, but the door didn't budge. Remembering that Lori had been here with an attitude, she set aside the keg and pulled on the door with both hands. It opened with a *POP!* and Vaughn landed on her ass on the cold, concrete floor. The keg clattered behind her. "Shit."

CHAPTER SIX

"**A**RE YOU OKAY?" Steps thundered down the stairs.

Before Vaughn could steady the empty keg, let alone stand, Justin skidded around the corner. She sagged, embarrassed. "I promise, it sounded worse than it was."

"It sounded fucking bad." Justin held out his hand. "The echo down here is legendary."

Vaughn swallowed, willing herself not to drool, then accepted Justin's hand and stood, lingering in his space a little longer than necessary. Captured by his gaze, she wanted to step closer, not away. "You smell like leather."

Justin let go of her hand. "Sorry."

"Don't be." She wiped her hands down the back of her pants and fidgeted, looking away as her cheeks burned. "It's nice."

He traced his fingers from her shoulder to her wrist. "You okay?"

She leaned toward him. She'd be better if he'd keep touching her.

More footsteps clattered on the stairs. "Did you beat someone to death with a keg?" Darryl appeared behind Justin with an impish grin. "And before you yell at me, for real. I was almost in the bar, and I heard that keg crash."

"Vaughn!" Another loud descent. "Are you okay?" Dylan skated around the corner, skirt hiked to their knees, assessed the situation, and grinned. "I told you not to throw any kegs unless Lori was around."

Vaughn laughed. Dylan's ability to defuse tension worked on her, even though she knew exactly what they were doing. "He deserves it. He slammed the door on the walk-in."

"And that bitch sealed tight as a chastity belt." Dylan sucked their teeth.

"You got it." Vaughn nodded. "Thank you. You guys are the best. I'm good though."

"At least let me check the handle and the seal," Justin said. "I am an engineer." He gestured to his shirt like a cheesy game show host.

"I'll get the keg, and then you can have at it, Rudolph Diesel."

"What?" Justin looked dazed.

"Rudolph Diesel? Mechanical Engineer?" Didn't engineers know this guy?

Justin still looked stunned.

"Invented the—"

"Diesel engine," Justin said at the same time as her. "Yeah."

"Justin," Darryl said.

"I know," Justin stretched out the word and squeezed his head. "No offense, but how do you know about Rudy?"

Vaughn chuckled. "When I was a kid, I heard a guy say diesel was pure testosterone. I googled it."

"Dangerous," Justin said.

"It was probably the most innocent thing I've ever overheard and looked up."

"Seriously, Justin," Darryl said.

"Yeah," Justin said.

Vaughn cocked her head. Apparently, these guys could have entire conversations with three words. Cute, but they'd spent enough time standing around. She had drinks to pour. "How's it looking up there, Dyl? Can you put a keg in reserve so I can change? I'm grimy."

"Absolutely, but, Darryl, go back upstairs." Dylan beamed at him. "And thanks for having my girl's back."

"Sure thing." Darryl turned to Vaughn. "I'm glad you're okay."

"Thanks." Vaughn escaped to their informal locker room. Usually, they stashed their things near the cash register, or in Cil's office, but the basement had a small room with two couches, a private bathroom with a shower, and a decent-sized closet where everyone kept a change of clothes and spare shoes. Vaughn grabbed a clean shirt and ducked into the bathroom.

She washed her hands and pulled off her sweater, sniffing it as she did. Justin had smelled lush. Vaughn didn't think she'd recover from the embarrassment if she'd reeked of dishwater or beer when they'd been close. Her sunshine-themed laundry detergent mostly held the bar funk at bay and reminded her of Justin's summer blue eyes. She leaned against the sink, needing to calm down before she embarrassed herself.

Except... she could tell when people were interested in her. Spending so much time in a bar had taught her the difference between someone who wanted to hold court, someone seeking sexual gratification, and someone with genuine interest. There were sparks between her and Justin from the moment they first spoke to each other. That definitely put him in the second category, but he seemed to lean toward the third, as well. That still didn't mean she should do anything about it. Lori seized any and every excuse to give her grief, her parents were probably expecting her to stay at their place again tonight since she'd driven Lori here, and Gusty didn't need any more reasons to tease her about her "Christmas gift." Though what a gift Justin would be.

Vaughn pulled out her ponytail, set the strands of tinsel aside, and dug her brush out from the toiletry bag she kept under the sink. She pulled the brush from top to bottom, getting out small tangles, and coaxing the strands to shine. Her hair was almost pretty. Almost. The natural color had potential, but where most people had a little variation, hers was flat. As shiny as she could make her hair, it was still a dull color between blonde and light brown, without even a hint of gold.

Not like Justin's. His hair was a warm brown near his head, but the further from the roots it got, the more golden it looked. It wasn't the result of dye growing out, either. There was no uniform place where the color suddenly changed. It simply did, and in the right light, it glimmered.

She swooped her hair over her shoulder and put it in a loose braid, while imagining what Justin's hair would look like hanging over her. Skimming her shoulders, her chest, her breasts. She secured the end of the braid and made a bow from the tinsel, then let her fingers trail down her abdomen, picturing Justin's. His chest against her back. His breath blowing against her neck. His hands cupping her breasts, teasing her nipples. She knew herself well enough that she could get herself off in a minute or two. Could he? Would his hands go exactly where she needed them?

If he walked into this room, would he instinctively be aggressive, but not so much that he missed her cues? Would he kiss her while he swirled a finger around her clit, and teased her entrance? Would he use one hand to drive her to her first orgasm, fast and a little sloppy? Or would he use both hands? Overwhelm her with his mouth on hers, then her neck, using his broad shoulders and chest to keep her steady as one hand worked her clit and the other penetrated, working in tandem to build the pressure, showing her that as much as he wanted to take the edge off for her, he also wanted to savor, explore, do more than get her off in a bathroom. Yes, she wanted much more than that.

But the two orgasms she delivered to herself would have to do. At the very least, they helped release some of her stress. She gave herself another moment to relax before she washed her hands and put herself back together, feeling better equipped to face whatever Lori would throw at her next.

When she finally left the locker room, she found Justin sitting on the bottom stair. She almost tripped over her own feet, wondering whether he could see what she'd been thinking in her unguarded expression.

He stood, hand out, as she stutter-stepped. "I didn't mean to startle you."

"No. I forgot you were down here. I shouldn't have taken so long."

Justin lifted a shoulder. "It wasn't even five minutes."

Vaughn's cheeks heated. It had been much longer in her mind. She cleared her throat. "Is the freezer door broken?"

"Oh." Justin gestured toward the walk-in. "No, but I want to show you something."

"Sure." She went to the walk-in and grabbed the handle. "Should I open it?"

"Not yet." Justin squatted and pointed at the bottom of the door. He launched into an explanation of seals and drafts and signs to watch for. All things she'd known forever.

Still, she liked the sound of his voice and that he'd waited to talk with her. She crouched next to him, making an active effort not to stare or inhale his scent.

"Okay." Vaughn waved in the area. "No draft. We're good." She stood, afraid if she stayed in that position she'd lean on him. Which would be nice, but probably awkward.

He straightened and opened the door. "You already know not to slam this but look." He pointed out the latch and the seal, telling her more things she knew, but in a way that showed he enjoyed figuring out how things work.

She stepped into the freezer and pointed to the top of the doorway. "I always check here to make sure the seal isn't flat."

Justin followed and stood close as he studied the area. "Good idea. Probably no one touches the frame there."

Vaughn had gotten lost watching his throat as he spoke and fought the urge to lean in. "Yeah."

Justin shuffled closer and stretched his arm, with his impossibly thick biceps, past her. "That's a good spot to check, too."

Vaughn barely turned her head, preferring to keep her focus on him. "Seems like it."

He dropped his arm and caught her gaze. "You already know all this, huh?"

Vaughn pressed her lips together and nodded.

"Thanks for indulging me. It was the best excuse I could think of to keep talking to you."

"I bet you're more creative than that."

He raised his eyebrows and leaned toward her, then back. "You should get out of here. Wouldn't want you to warm up the beer."

She blinked a few times, then laughed. "That was unexpectedly corny. But I liked it."

"Good." He took her hand and left the walk-in, shutting it gently. "The tinsel bartender keeps saying I should come back. Do you want me to?"

"Yeah." Vaughn squeezed his hand, hoping he'd get the message that she meant it. "Come back tomorrow if you want."

Justin's eyes roved over her. "I want."

Maybe it had been his mention of Cheyenne that emboldened her, or the fantasy she'd allowed herself in the bathroom. Either way, she didn't second-guess herself as she leaned into his space and kissed his cheek. "Good."

He turned his head and kissed her back, somehow holding her close even though he only held her hand.

"Vaughn!" Dylan shouted from upstairs. "Can you bring up a bottle of Korbel brandy?"

The last thing she wanted to do was stop the kiss, but if she didn't answer Dylan, they'd come down. She pulled away from Justin to avoid shouting in his ear. "Anything else?"

"Nope!"

"Be up in a sec!"

Justin cleared his throat and loosened his grip on her. "Brandy goes fast, huh?"

Vaughn smiled. "Tom and Jerry season." She reluctantly let go of his hand to retrieve the bottle from a row of nearby shelves. "Cil says it's better than eggnog, but I'd rather have brandy straight. Maybe with lemonade."

"My grandmother likes a cold Brandy Alexander."

"Boozy milkshake. Solid choice."

Justin smiled, gestured toward the stairs, and followed Vaughn as she climbed them.

When she got to the top, she waited for him before turning off the basement lights and closing the door. "We open tomorrow at three."

"I'll be here."

She lifted her chin, and he took the hint, giving her a chaste but lingering kiss.

CHAPTER SEVEN

"**V**AUGHN," DYLAN WAVED an empty bottle at her. "Lori's crew killed the Blanton's Black, and they want more."

"He sold a $350 bottle?" Stunned, Vaughn put a hand on her hip. She suspected that Lori had likely given his friends a steep discount, but living in the afterglow of Justin's kisses dimmed her concern.

"Seems like it."

"There's another one in the party room. I'll get it." Vaughn skirted around Dylan and headed to the spare room, where they had a small bar and sometimes held private events.

The room was unlocked, with the lights on. Sheryl sat on a stool, arms stretched out with her back to the polished mahogany counter. Lori stood between her legs, his hands on her hips, and his face pushed against her throat.

"I'll make this quick," Vaughn said as she marched to the bar.

"What?" Lori looked around as though surprised by the lights. "Why are you here? This room is closed."

"Your friends need more Blanton's Black." Vaughn worked to keep her gaze on the bottles of liquor, scanning for the one she wanted.

"They can drink something else," Lori said. "Sheryl and I need some time."

"It'll only take a second." Vaughn crouched behind the bar, searching a lower cabinet for the bottle.

"Lori," Sheryl whispered. "Let them have it. We're good."

"It's your favorite, baby," he crooned.

"It's fine." Sheryl cleared her throat. "Vaughn." A bottle scraped across the counter. "It's here. Take it."

"I'm sorry?" Vaughn rose and turned to face Lori and Sheryl.

Sheryl nudged an open bottle toward Vaughn. With her other hand, she found the top and passed it over as well. "We've had enough. Go on and serve it to the guys."

Vaughn pinched the bridge of her nose. Maybe Lori didn't know. Maybe Cil had started the full bottle policy after Lori had moved. She picked it up and checked how much they'd drunk before setting it back on the counter. "Lori, we sell this by the bottle."

He shrugged. "And?"

"You opened it. Now I have to charge $88 a shot. We'll be stuck with an open bottle."

Lori hugged Sheryl closer to him. "I don't care what you charge them. They'll finish the bottle."

"You buy this bottle. I don't have a lot of faith in your crew since two of your guys skipped out on their bill."

Lori looked at her over Sheryl's shoulder. "I told you I'd handle it. Take the bottle and go."

Vaughn corked the bourbon, letting her glare burn into Lori as she sifted through dozens of scathing responses before settling on the one she figured would make the most impact. "Cil checks the books every morning. If you actually want Crawford's to kill him, giving away two $350 bottles oughta do it." She grabbed the bottle by the neck and stalked out. She stormed to the bar, doing her best not to upset customers, but knowing her fuse was frayed, she stuck to smiles and waves.

"Everyone has a fresh whatever," Dylan said. "The tables are caught up, too. I'm gonna go help Cheyenne move the food. Those boys are gonna play us some songs."

"Okay." Vaughn stowed the bottle and looked around. Her gaze drifted to the stage, where Justin arranged drums. He glanced up and smiled at her. Returning his smile, she watched the guys for a moment, letting her temper subside. She'd deal with Lori later. There were better places for her energy.

"Is it clichéd to fall for a musician?" Cheyenne filled a glass with water and sipped it.

"I hope not," Vaughn said.

A few seats away, Gusty laughed. His wife bumped him with her shoulder but didn't hide her broad smile.

"You stop it." Cheyenne pulled another draft and set it in front of Gusty. "I'm not gonna recreate music videos."

Vaughn shook her head. "That's not why he's laughing."

"She's right." Gusty drank from his fresh beer. "For the record, people should enjoy their Christmas gifts."

"Hear, hear!" His wife clinked her glass to his.

Vaughn raised her gaze to the ceiling and shook her head, as if to ask the bar gods why this guy was still going on about gifts.

"Hello, everybody."

The striking man who'd spoken into the microphone won the attention of the room. He wore a T-shirt similar to Justin's, except his identified him as a teacher. He kept the banter short, offering to play carols, and showed obvious relief when the crowd booed the idea. "Rock-and-roll then."

Justin brought his drumsticks down and quickly settled into a beat. He winked at Vaughn.

She smiled and turned back to her customers.

"You ever find another bottle of Blanton's?"

"Yeah." Vaughn zeroed in on the man and wracked her brain for his name. "Let's settle up on the other bottle first." She searched the system for his tab. No matter how she searched—by stool location, the man's description, name of the alcohol, even Lori's name—nothing came up. "Sorry, what's your name?"

"You don't remember your Uncle Steven?"

Vaughn gave him a blank face. "You spell it with a v or a ph?"

He narrowed his eyes. "V. But I doubt it's in there. Lori said he'd handle it."

She didn't have to ask Lori to know Steven wasn't lying. What she'd suspected had become clear. "Lori got that bottle, but I'm opening a tab on this one. It's $88 a drink. You paying with Visa or Mastercard?"

Steven laughed. "No. Lori said I was fine."

Vaughn leaned a hip against her work counter. "Fine for the last bottle. This one's new. $88 a drink. Take it or leave it."

He stood. "Lori said you had a mouth on you. I'll get this settled."

Vaughn leaned forward on the bar. "I don't give a shit what Lori says. You don't talk to me or my staff like that. You want any more drinks tonight, you pay for them, or you go somewhere else."

"Where's Lori?" Steven's tone had turned stony.

"Trying to fuck Sheryl in the backroom."

He called Vaughn a "rude bitch" and pushed through the crowd.

"Did he say what I think he said?" Dylan asked.

"Sure did." Vaughn cleared the space where he'd been sitting, scrubbing away all traces of Steven and his shitty vibe. She gestured to someone standing nearby to take the seat.

"Want me to expel him?"

"Hoping Lori will." She took the order for the new person and got their drink.

"This should be fun."

"You know it." Vaughn pulled the garbage can from where Lori had been working and dragged it into Cil's office. She found a spare and brought it out, lined with a fresh bag.

"I woulda emptied that for you," Cheyenne said.

Vaughn shook her head. "I'm pretty sure it's full of the bottles Lori gave away."

"What?" Cheyenne finally looked frustrated by the tinsel she'd been shedding. She wiped her hands down both arms and stomped her feet. "He's been giving away drinks?"

Dylan handed Vaughn a long report from the register. "I think you're right. I asked the last two guys if Lori had given them a deal. They said he told them to come by and leave their wallets at home."

"Son of a bitch!" Vaughn stalked the length of the bar and back, then pulled Dylan and Cheyenne back from the customers. "He's been bullying me and Cil all week about selling Crawford's, then about closing, and now that asshole is actively sabotaging us."

"Close Crawford's?" Cheyenne asked.

Dylan paled. "Vaughn, this place is my career. Cil and I made a plan."

Vaughn closed her eyes to calm herself before she spoke. She'd never meant to worry them; she'd wanted to vent. "I know. We aren't closing. He and I also have a plan. Everything will keep running, even beyond Cil. It's what he wants."

"Does Lori know what Cil wants?" Cheyenne asked.

"Fuck if I know." Vaughn fiddled with the end of her braid. "He probably doesn't give a shit." She dropped her hair and blinked fast, a new realization hitting her. "How am I going to tell my grandfather what Lori's done?"

Dylan pulled her into a tight hug. "You've got this. We'll back you up."

Cheyenne curled around them. "Most of the community, too. Businesses, regulars. This bar is bigger than Lori's temper."

"Thanks, guys." Vaughn squeezed them tighter before letting go. They'd started as co-workers, but it hadn't taken long for the three of them to bond. Even without their reassurances, Vaughn knew in her bones Cheyenne and Dylan would stand with her, just as she would with them. "Promise to bail me out if I get arrested for assaulting him."

Cheyenne laughed.

"You got it." Dylan said.

"You guys okay over there?" Gusty called out.

"We're fine," Vaughn said.

"I'm also willing to bail you out, and that's even if you don't refill my wife," he said.

69

Cheyenne made a rum and cola. "At least she's drinking something with some heft to it, Mr. Natty Light." She gently set the glass in front of Gusty's wife. "Sorry for taking so long."

The woman tinkled a laugh. "I barely finished the first one. He's just being ornery."

Gusty sat up straighter. "It's part of my charm."

Vaughn gave a watery laugh as Dylan released her, patting her back.

"We have the orneriest man in the Midwest on our side. We'll be fine," they said.

A field whistle echoed through the bar, again stopping all conversation, even the music. Lori stood at the edge of the hallway, nostrils flared, hands at his waist.

"Bring it," Vaughn said.

CHAPTER EIGHT

VAUGHN TILTED HER head, assessing Lori's posture. Would he drag a foot across the ground before he charged? The moments she'd spent with her people–her friends–had refueled her. Whatever he had for her now, she was ready.

Lori stomped toward her, one hand fiddling with his belt. He stopped several feet from the bar.

Sheryl tugged one of his arms, her coat and purse dangling from one shoulder. "We should go. Let's go," she stage whispered frantically.

He brushed her off. "You shaking down my friends, Vaughn?" he bellowed. "You know better than to embarrass me."

"I know better than to steal from the family business." Vaughn spoke as loud as Lori had, her voice clear and steady. "Do you?"

Someone let out an *"oof"* in the otherwise silent room.

Lori's eyes bulged, and his cheeks reddened. He sneered and opened his mouth. Then snapped it shut and pushed his way toward the bar.

Sheryl trailed behind him before veering off and gesturing toward a smug-looking Steven, who blocked the hallway to the private room.

Vaughn glanced at the stage, willing them to play another song.

Justin lifted from his seat, a questioning look on his face.

She twirled her finger in the air, and he resumed a beat. The rest of the band quickly joined, filling the bar with music, and giving Vaughn and Lori a shred of privacy.

Vaughn turned back toward Lori, expecting him to come behind the counter.

Instead, he shoved himself between two customers and pressed his hands into the marble as he leaned toward her. "How dare you put me in a spot like that?" he seethed.

Vaughn glared right back and held his gaze, firm despite how angry she was that he'd defended his own shady honor and not his father. "How dare you treat this business like trash? The thing your father spent his life building. The thing that kept a roof over your head and put you through school."

Lori reared back. "How dare I? How dare *I*?" His bark drowned out the music for a moment.

The people closest to the bar were focused on Vaughn and Lori, not the live music, their drinks, or even the people they were with. All eyes were on the unfolding feud.

Vaughn reached across the counter and gripped his shirt, pulling him close, not wanting everyone to hear her. "You're trying to tear down his life's work." He tried to wrench her hand away, but she twisted her fingers into the worn fabric even tighter. "The thing that gives purpose to his days. You're beating him up over it. And when he's too tired to fight, when he finally gives in and lets you take away the most constant thing he has, it will kill him." She let go and stood straight. "It probably doesn't matter to you, but I won't ever forgive you for that."

Lori looked like Vaughn had hit him with an empty keg. "I-I love him," he stammered. "I'm trying to protect him."

"You have a shit way of showing it." Vaughn crossed her arms.

He curled his hands into fists and pounded the bar. "I'm saving him! This *bar* is killing him!"

Tired of the theatrics, Vaughn shook her head. "You can't be serious."

"I am!"

"What the fuck are you talking about?" Vaughn asked.

"Every time I call, he's tired. Every time I see him, he looks older."

Dylan cleared their throat. "He is older, Lori. That's how living works."

"He's tired because you call him after nine." She was done with Lori living in a separate reality. He didn't deserve explanations, and probably wouldn't listen, but Cil deserved better from all of them. "He's usually in bed by ten. When you tell him to expect a call, he makes himself coffee after dinner."

"I call him late to send him home from work." Lori knocked on the bar. "Why are you letting him drink coffee at night? His heart'll explode!"

"Let him?" Vaughn smacked her forehead. It was as though Lori had no idea that he'd gotten his bullheadedness from Cil. "Are you serious? The day he *lets* me tell him what to do is the day he gets a tattoo on his face."

"Dad wants a tattoo?" Lori's expression screwed up in confusion and anger, his complexion getting ruddier.

Vaughn rolled her eyes. "Get back here. I'm not having this conversation in front of the whole city."

Lori huffed and pushed off the counter. He muttered apologies to the people he'd displaced in his tirade and trudged behind the bar.

"I don't care about Ann Arbor. I care about how my dad is well into his seventies and still working."

"He isn't," Vaughn said.

"Bullshit," Lori scoffed.

"She's not lying," Dylan said. "If you'd get out of your own way and pay attention, you'd know."

"Gusty," Lori barked while glaring at Vaughn. "How many nights a week is my dad here?"

"Two. Maybe three."

"What?" Lori whirled around and leaned toward Gusty. "Three?"

"Only when the Blackhawks are playing. We watch the first period together."

"Then he goes home," Vaughn said. "And either watches the rest of the game from bed or drinks coffee, waiting for your call." She gave a patron with a full beer the stink eye and pointed toward the band, willing the man to be less obvious about listening in.

"Are you serious?"

Gusty nodded. "Dead serious."

"He helps with inventory when we get deliveries, and he goes over the books with me every morning," Dylan said. "That's it." They leaned against the counter, eyebrow raised at someone who watched the conversation like it was a tennis match.

Vaughn squeezed Dylan's shoulder and refocused on Lori. "And he only does that to make sure Crawford's is in good shape when you and Mom inherit it."

"What?"

"Sounds like he wants to pass on a success." Gusty sipped his beer.

"And you want to take that from him." Vaughn got into her uncle's space, backing him into the cash register. "He's spent years in this community, years building this business. It's his lifeline. Encourage him to retire. Don't invalidate what he's done with his life."

"I don't... how can you say that?" Lori pushed back his shoulders and puffed out his chest. "I want my father to have a comfortable life. He's spent most of it on his feet. I want him to reap the rewards."

"He does." Vaughn took a step back. "When he sees familiar faces here. When people invite him to their events. When new businesses introduce themselves because he's Cillian Fucking Hayes, the man who gave this neighborhood roots." Vaughn's gaze trailed to a photo hanging next to the cash register. Cil referred to it as the "class photo," a picture taken every year of him and his staff. He always looked proud in them. "He's not the type to sell and move to a beachfront condo in Florida."

"And thank God for that," Dylan said. "We need him as much as he needs this bar."

Lori pushed past Vaughn and pointed at Dylan. "See! You need him!"

"Not to sling drinks and haul kegs!" Vaughn shook her fists near her head, fighting her deep need to shake the shit out of Lori. "He's the cornerstone of Ann Arbor hospitality. We need him because he's the proof small businesses thrive here."

Lori spun and faced Vaugh, nostrils flaring again. "You've turned my father into a fucking mascot, and you expect me to be okay with it?"

Vaughn reached into a bin with empty bottles, lifted one above her head and slammed it into the ground, shattering the bottle and screaming so loud everything in the bar stopped. Except Cheyenne, who stepped behind her and wrapped Vaughn in her arms.

She shook as she glared at her uncle. "Get the fuck out."

Lori blinked a few times before shifting his gaze from the shattered glass to Vaughn. "What?"

"You don't deserve to be here. Fucking leave!" Vaughn lashed the words at him.

Lori remained in place, his eyes wide. He shook his head so fast his jowls swayed. "Vaughn. I'm sorry."

"If you were, you wouldn't be sabotaging him."

"I'm not—"

Vaughn stomped her foot. "I don't want him to die," she and Lori shouted at the same time.

CHAPTER NINE

C HEYENNE RELEASED HER hold on Vaughn and sobbed. It was the only sound in the room. "None of us want to lose Cil."

Vaughn blinked fast, fighting back tears, but gave in when she saw Lori's glassy eyes. She pressed her face into his chest and hugged him, gripping tightly as they both cried.

Behind her, Dylan sniffled, and a broom swept shards of glass across the floor.

"Oh my God," Cheyenne sobbed. "PLAY WHITESNAKE."

Justin launched into the chorus of "Here I Go Again," his singer catching on fast as the rest of the guys picked up the song. The bar broke out in cheers, some people even singing along. After the next verse, the band transitioned to another 80s hit, playing a medley for a few minutes before transitioning to another one of their songs.

Vaughn's tears turned to laugher as she recognized the tunes and the enthusiastic reactions from her customers. Dylan had cleaned up the broken bottle, and everyone danced, the pressure valve in the room released.

Vaughn dragged over a leather stool with a low upholstered back. She patted the seat and gestured for Lori to sit. "This is where Cil sits when he's here."

"He's our cruise director," Cheyenne said.

Lori gripped Vaughn's hand. "I'm sorry."

Vaughn nodded. "Go easy on him. The rest of us do."

Lori squeezed Vaughn's hand and gave her a hangdog expression. "I had no idea. I'll do better."

Vaughn spent the next few minutes walking Lori through schedules and plans, showing him exactly how involved Cil was in the day-to-day operations. "He's the King of Ann Arbor. Lots of respect and cool hats, but most of his work is ceremonial."

Lori leaned back on the stool and gave a deep chuckle. "My dad *is* a king. And his hat game is strong."

Vaughn smiled and gave him a side hug, excited they'd found common ground.

A man waving a card in the air pushed his way to the counter. "I got unlimited funds now. You gotta let me back in."

"Can I help you?" Cheyenne asked.

Vaughn zeroed in on the man and shook her head. She knew that beanie. "You're an unlimited asshole, and I don't mind kicking you out twice. Doesn't matter how much money you have."

"Oh!" Cheyenne shooed the man away. "I know who you are. Once you get kicked out, you can't come back. Them's the rules."

"Buh-bye." Dylan waved.

The guy slapped his black card on the bar. "I'm an asshole with money, wench! Get me a Molson!"

"I got this." Lori hopped off the stool and leaned against the bar. "You heard the lady. Leave."

"You can't do anything about it." The guy pushed his beanie up his forehead.

"Watch me." Lori flicked the credit card off the bar, forcing the guy to bend down for it, and met him on the other side. "You got it yet?" He sneered at the guy, grabbed him by the elbows, and steered him through the crowd toward the door.

"That was smooth," Cheyenne said. "I'm impressed."

Dylan crossed their arms. "Very efficient for Lori."

Vaughn grinned. "*That's* my uncle."

The closer they got to the door, the more the guy struggled.

Vaughn followed, phone in hand, in case she needed to call a ride for the guy, or the police.

The guy almost got the upper hand on Lori when they reached the threshold. Lori had let go of one of his arms to hold the door open, and the guy spun.

81

"You can't kick a paying customer out!"

"You never paid in the first place," Vaughn said.

He waved the card. "I can pay!" He burped in Lori's face.

Lori pushed himself against the door, waving away the air in his face. "You gotta ride, buddy?"

"What do you care?" The guy moved toward Lori.

Vaughn realized Lori was keeping the guy on his feet and waved for Dylan or Cheyenne to come help.

The guy burped again, then bent over and vomited on Lori's legs. "Ope." He wiped his hands down Lori's pants.

"It's alright, buddy. Stop. They'll wash."

"My bad," the guy said before heaving again. He gripped Lori's legs as he spilled his dinner on the floor. When he finally righted himself, he tugged on Lori's pants, sending them to rest in the puddle of sick.

CHAPTER TEN

VAUGHN GAVE LORI a wide-eyed look, then darted her gaze to the ceiling as Lori looked down.

"Long shirt, Vaughn. I'm covered." He leaned against the door, staring at his pants. "If it wasn't part of my moral code not to hit drunk people—"

The guy swayed and Sheryl rushed him, pushing the man fully out of the bar and Lori's grasp. "Go toss your beer in the gutter!"

"Is that... two stags... fucking on his underwear?" someone asked.

Sheryl shrugged out of her coat, pushed it against Lori's waist, and turned wild eyes toward the tables near the door. "There's a band playing. Pay attention to them!"

As though he'd heard Sheryl, the lead singer spoke from the stage. "Show's up here, friends. Who's got a request?"

Cheyenne materialized with pitchers of steaming water. "Oh no, I didn't realize how bad he got you."

"Don't worry about me." Lori held Sheryl's coat against his legs. "We gotta rinse it away and salt the area."

"Got it." Dylan handed Vaughn a bag of sand. "I'll get more water."

Vaughn balanced the bag against her hip. "We have spare clothes downstairs, but I don't know about shoes."

"He should take that drunk motherfucker's." Sheryl flicked her hand at the man hunched over the curb, using his beanie to wipe his mouth.

"I'm impressed to see you channeling your rage at someone besides me," Lori said.

Sheryl glared at him. "You deserve all my rage. But that guy's a douchebag."

Vaughn laughed outright. "Thanks for defending the bar, Sheryl."

She nodded. "Sorry you have to clean this up."

"Sher, go inside," Lori said, "while I figure out how to get out of this mess without tracking it in."

The tiny woman held her ground.

Lori flicked the coat he held in front of himself. "I don't want you to catch a chill. Please, baby."

She put a hand on her hip. "You're welcome." She turned toward the room. "Gonna go to the ladies' room." She wove between the tables, glaring at people who dared watch her.

Vaughn, Dylan, and Cheyenne took turns ferrying hot water to rinse off the entry and then coated it with sand. Vaughn made Lori stand in the doorway until they'd rinsed the sidewalk clean. Dylan produced a pair of disposable gloves, and Lori donned them to untie his shoes and step out of his pants. They dumped more water on them before Lori decided the pants were dumpster bound and salvaged his belt and wallet.

"How did he get your jeans down so easy?" Cheyenne asked.

Lori turned Rudolph red. "I was in the back with Sheryl. Steven interrupted, and I got pissed." He lifted his shoulders. "I didn't button up or hook my belt."

Cheyenne belly laughed, pulled tinsel from her sweater, and threw it at him before threading her arm through Vaughn's and returning to the bar.

The college kid from earlier shouted, "Can I get a picture for my aunt?"

Lori shook his ass, which led to whistles, catcalls, and comments about shrinkage shouted at him as he made his way behind the bar and down to the break room to rummage for clean pants.

"Vaughn." Sheryl popped up at the end of the bar. "Do you mind if I take Lori home? Losing his jeans is kinda my fault and I feel bad."

Vaughn nodded. "Pull your car around back. I'll let him know you're waiting."

"Thanks." Sheryl pushed away from the counter, then came back. "You deserve an apology from him. I'll make sure you get it."

Vaughn reached over and squeezed Sheryl's hand. "He and I are straight now. Focus on the apology he owes *you*. We both know he's better than the way he's been lately."

Sheryl swallowed and nodded. "I never would've showed up tonight otherwise. At least not like this."

"I get it." Vaughn smiled. "Go get him."

"Merry Christmas, Vaughn."

Vaughn flicked the garland that hung above them, setting small bells tinkling. "You, too."

The rest of the night felt like a good house party. The band took a short break, during which Justin made a beeline for Vaughn, asking her half a dozen times if she was okay. By the time he'd resumed his seat behind the drums, Vaughn had moved him squarely into the "has genuine interest" category and had fun pondering what she'd do about it.

The second set the band played was carefree and fun in a way the first one hadn't been. It was full of classic songs, a few silly carols, and more requests from the audience. People sang along and danced, with laughter flowing as freely as the beer.

Gusty danced with his wife until she collapsed on her stool, laughing and flushed. He settled their bill and helped her into her coat. When he knocked on the counter, Vaughn raised her eyebrows. "I know. That's not my usual style, but I wanted to make sure I said thank you for opening tonight. This was fun."

"All of it?" Vaughn asked.

"Fights are always better when you're a spectator." Gusty winked and opened his wallet. He laid three crisp one-hundred-dollar bills on the bar. "Welp. You three are the tits. Get yourselves something nice."

"Gusty!"

"Merry Christmas!" his wife sang. She pulled Gusty away, wrapping her arms around his waist.

"Crankiest man in Michigan, and the most generous," Dylan said.

Vaughn hip-checked him, feeling lighter than she had since Lori'd arrived. "We must be doing something right." She tucked the bills in the tip jar, knowing Cheyenne would light up when she saw Gusty's gift.

The band stayed as Crawford's emptied, taking their time packing gear and nursing drinks. Cheyenne swept the floor as Vaughn wiped down tables and flipped the chairs on top of them. They'd almost made it to the stage when Chris interrupted them.

"Hey, Vaughn." He held a pitcher full of bills toward her. "Since it's kinda my fault the pukey dude left without paying his bill, I talked the guys into giving you our tips to cover his bill."

Vaughn blinked a few times and looked at Justin. He jutted his chin toward Chris.

"Keep your tips. We've got it."

Chris shook his head. "No. Darryl says I put my ass where it doesn't belong too often, and you shouldn't pay the price." He screwed up his face and rolled his eyes. "And that jack-off is right. Please take this."

Vaughn pressed her lips together to hold back her smile. She looked past Chris. "You guys okay with this? People were generous tonight."

"Absolutely," the singer said.

"We're gonna make him work it off anyway," Darryl said.

"This is a lot of work already, buddy," Chris shouted over his shoulder.

Vaughn caught Justin's eye and raised her eyebrows. He nodded.

Vaughn accepted the money. "Thank you."

Chris rubbed his head and sighed. "Yeah. Thanks for letting us play."

"Are you kidding?" Cheyenne asked. "You guys were great. You were awesome before all hell broke loose, and then after, you guys lifted the mood. You made the night."

"That's why we do it." Darryl lifted the cases with his keyboards and walked toward them. "It's fun to be part of something like this. Thanks for having us."

"You guys can play here anytime." Vaughn made a mental note to make sure she reminded Justin the next time she saw him. She liked him *and* his music. Filling the bar with both would be a nice addition.

Darryl and Chris carried gear out, their singer and Justin following close behind.

"Hang on, Justin." Vaughn left her cleaning supplies at the table and caught up to him. She pulled the tinsel bow from the end of her braid and tied it around his wrist. "See you tomorrow?"

"Hell yes." He kissed her cheek.

She wanted to return the kiss but didn't trust herself to keep it chaste, even with Cheyenne and Dylan watching her. She pressed her cheek to his and brushed her lips against him. "Don't forget."

"Impossible." He squeezed her hand. "Open at three, right?"

"Yeah."

"I'll be here."

"Good." Vaughn watched him leave, before joining Cheyenne.

"Go catch him," she said. "Dyl and I got this."

Vaughn shook her head. "He'll be back."

When she and Cheyenne finished cleaning the main area, Vaughn returned to the bar for her favorite bottle of whiskey and three glasses. She settled on the stool where Gusty had sat most of the evening and poured a drink for herself, Dylan, and Cheyenne. She set each glass on top of a hundred-dollar bill. "Shots up!"

Cheyenne sat next to Vaughn, while Dylan stayed behind the counter and produced a small plate of bao—with the magic pork—and napkins.

Dylan lifted a glass. "Here's to remembering the best parts of today and letting the rest go."

"Amen." Cheyenne clinked her glass against Dylan's, then Vaughn's, and drank deep. "What's this?" she asked as she set her glass down next to the cash.

"Merry Christmas from Gusty and his Mrs.," Vaughn said.

Cheyenne leaned back, a grin lighting her face. "He wasn't kidding about wanting us to enjoy our presents, was he?"

Vaughn laughed as she topped off their glasses.

They sat together for a few minutes, eating bao and talking about the evening. They were laughing over Lori's pants when the front door creaked open and Justin stepped inside, followed by a biting wind.

"Your intuition is spot on." Cheyenne gave Vaughn a smile worthy of a music video.

He closed the door and shivered against it before he approached the bar. "I noticed a car idling outside and didn't want you to have to walk out alone."

"Beige Camry?" Dylan asked.

Justin nodded.

"That's my sister. Want a ride, Cheyenne?"

She hopped off the stool. "Only if she doesn't mind tinsel."

"She's a teacher. Glitter." Dylan made jazz hands. "Everywhere. Always. Tinsel will fit right in."

"Perf."

Dylan passed Cheyenne's coat over the counter, tossed the empty plate and napkins in the garbage, and washed and put away the glasses and the whiskey bottle.

"Efficient, Dyl," Vaughn said.

"Always." They flashed their eyebrows and glided out from behind the bar. "I'll lock this door if you want to lock the back, Vaughn."

She nodded and watched her friends, a smile playing on her lips.

Dylan turned off the lights before slipping out the door, leaving Vaughn and Justin in the glow from the twinkle lights wrapped in the boughs above the bar.

"They leave you here with strange men often?"

Vaughn laughed. "That's the job description." She slid off her stool and stood next to him. "But Dylan is a ninth dan in Judo and gives our staff regular self-defense lessons."

"Ninth dan?"

"Black belt."

Justin pushed his hand through his hair. "Shit. *They* should walk you out."

"Dylan knows I can handle myself." Vaughn tilted her head, wondering if Justin would say more. When he didn't, she gave him a lifeline. "And they won't leave until they see me drive by."

"You have a good crew."

Vaughn nodded. "So do you." She walked behind the counter and gestured for him to follow. "That tip jar was pretty heavy. You sure you don't want to at least split it between your band and Crawford's?"

"Nope. We were planning to practice in a cold ass storage unit. This was a cherry set up. No tips needed."

"I parked in the back," Vaughn said, tired of small talk. "If you're gonna walk me to my car, I can drive you back to yours."

"No need."

"It's almost down to zero degrees out there." Vaughn rubbed her hands along his arms in a thinly veiled masquerade to warm him when all she wanted was to touch him.

"I'll live." His voice was husky, his eyes heated.

"Come on." Vaughn rang the bell at the register as she walked past. She turned off the holiday lights and took Justin down the hallway to the back door, where her coat hung on an ancient rack.

"Wait." He tapped her hand. "I stepped in it back there."

Vaughn looked at his feet. "We didn't rinse away all the spew?"

Justin thumped his foot. "I'm so bad at this." He looked her in the eye. "The sidewalk is clear. I meant metaphorically."

"Okay."

"Walking you to your car was an excuse. I know you can handle yourself, and I should've known, especially after everything tonight, that your crew has your back."

Vaughn crossed her arms. "They do."

"I'm sorry if I sounded like a douchebag who thinks you're helpless. You're amazing and I want to kiss you again. I should've thought—"

Vaughn pulled his mouth to hers and kissed him the way she'd wanted to kiss him when Dylan interrupted them in the basement. "You're forgiven."

"Excellent." Justin pulled her flush against him, backing her into the wall, and kissed her with even more intensity.

Enjoying his kiss and the feel of him, she slid her leg along his, hooking her knee around his firm thigh, making him groan. "Are you parked nearby?"

Justin kissed her again. "No."

"Let me take you somewhere." Vaughn kissed him as she dug through her pockets for her keys. When she closed her fingers around them, she broke away. "Go outside so I can turn on the alarm."

Vaughn felt the rumble in his chest as Justin kissed her and then let her go. "Okay." He slipped out the door. "Hurry," he said as he closed it.

Vaughn had never entered the alarm code faster. When she stepped into the alley, a gust of wind hit that was so strong Justin had to help her close the door. Once she had it secured, she spun in his arms and hit the unlock button for her car. "Thanks for your help."

"Didn't want the alarm to go off."

"Thoughtful." Vaughn rubbed her hands up his chest. "You're a really nice shield against the wind, but we should get in the car."

His gaze burned her up before he dropped his head and rubbed his nose along her jaw and up to her ear. He shivered as he bore the brunt of another gust. "Okay."

They dashed to the car and Vaughn turned it on, cranking the heat as they buckled up.

Justin angled toward her. "Where do you want to take me?"

"Home."

A smile bloomed across his face. "You sure?"

She stretched across the car and whispered, "Yes," before she kissed him. She pulled him toward her and by the time they came up for air, Justin was almost in her seat.

"Whose?" he asked.

"Yours."

"You sure?"

She grasped his chin with her thumb and fore-finger and popped a quick kiss on his lips. "Without a doubt." He was the Christmas gift she had every intention of enjoying.

ACKNOWLEDGMENTS

This novella would not have been possible without the support of my writing community. They cheered me on and kept me going, even when I was whining so much, I annoyed myself. Special thanks to Kitty, Angela, Cat, and Sita. Stephanie and Jem helped me out in a pinch with 11th hour referrals that were perfect. Thank you to Tora Brumalis for her sensitivity read. This is the first time I worked with a sensitivity reader who was not a friend-of-a-friend, and she was wonderful. Thank you to my amazing cover designer, Suzanna, who did double duty this go round and helped me name this novella.

Thank you to my readers. Your support, and being able to share these characters with you, is a privilege that I will forever be grateful for.

Finally, to my husband and kids, I'm sorry for all the dirty looks I gave you while writing this book. I hope you love me anyway. You guys are the best.

ABOUT THE AUTHOR

ELAINE REED

Elaine lives in South Carolina's Low Country. When she isn't writing, she can be found exploring Charleston, taking in live music and searching for shark teeth on the beach with her family.

www.elaine-writes.com

Sign up for her newsletter: https://www.elaine-writes.com/newsletter/

Facebook https://www.facebook.com/elainereedwrites

Twitter https://twitter.com/_elainewrites

Instagram https://www.instagram.com/_elainewrites/

TikTok https:/www.tiktok.com/@_elainewrites

If this book made you feel something, whether love or hate, please consider leaving a review where you purchased it, on your blog, or another book site. Share your thoughts on social media. If you believe the book has value and is worth sharing, would you take a few seconds to let your friends know about it? If it they like it, they'll be grateful to you. As will I.

MORE BY ELAINE

The Girl U Want

Sue Douglas has no time for men. At least not any more men. She scored her dream job as a publicist for an up-and-coming rock band, but they're putting her through her paces:

> The bass player despises her
> The lead singer lusts for her
> The band manager dumped a
> career-ending secret on her
> The band's record company is deter-
> mined to see her fail

And if she even stumbles, she could lose everything.

In the middle of it all, she meets *the* man. The one she wants in her schedule. He sees the mayhem of her life but refuses to let her go. He says he'll only take her spare time, but there's no time on a tour that will make or break her as a publicist.

Have Love Will Travel

Sue Douglas has no time for crap. At least not any more crap. She's trying to turn her dream job as a publicist into her dream career, but it's more complicated than it looks:

> *Her bass player is still a pain in the ass*
> *Her lead singer is still too flirty*
> *Their record company is still throwing shade her way.*
> *But then, there's Adam.*

Through it all, he's there. Willing to take whatever pieces of time she can give him. But his love softens her, and in her world where power is access, softness is a weakness. Now Sue has one very big puzzle to solve: how to cherish the soft without losing all she's worked for.

A Drummer Boy for Christmas

If Vaughn Williams had a dollar for every argument her uncle had started during his holiday visit, she'd be able to open her own bar. Which would come in handy since her uncle seems dead set on closing the one her family owns. Shutting the fifty-year-old business would put Vaughn and half a dozen others out of work and break her grandfather's heart.

Determined to stop the arguing, keep herself busy, and maybe even prove a point to her uncle, Vaughn opens the bar on Christmas night. It becomes a haven for their neighborhood, and even calms her uncle. Best of all, Vaughn meets a man who seems interested in more than flirting over a few drinks.

Vaughn's ready for a relaxed night with an intriguing man, but her uncle keeps finding ways to start fights. Will he get the blowout he wants? Or will Vaughn get to enjoy her new friend?

Take a Chance on Me

After two years on the road with his band, Justin Arnold is finally home. All he wants to do is hang out and record the next album. But the producer is ruining all the songs, and his bass player's bid to be on a reality show has cameras constantly in the way. Thankfully, Justin can escape with Vaughn, his friend with benefits.

Ever since they met, Vaughn Williams hasn't been able to say no to Justin. He's a great partner...when he's home. Suddenly he wants to date, but she's not convinced they'll be able to make it work. Especially when another tour will take him away from her again.

So when he's offered a leading role in a reality dating show with his bandmate, Vaughn encourages him to go for it. He can help his band, she can focus on running her bar, and no one gets hurt.

It's win-win for both of them. Except the show isn't what it seems and no matter what Vaughn does, she can't shake the feeling that she's made one hell of a mistake.

Frustrated with everything, Justin is ready to quit the show and write off Vaughn. Until he walks into her bar one day and sees that he might still be on her mind.

Champagne Supernova
A Word's Fail Me Holiday Novella

Autumn Powell believes the right pair of shoes can change her life, and she's determined to start the New Year on the right foot. Unfortunately, the pair she's wearing isn't hers.

Chester Quartermain has a great eye for detail, and the woman before him is a masterpiece. Too bad she's wearing his stolen shoe design.

Getting her out of them might have to be his New Year's Resolution.

Caught Up in You
A Word's Fail Me Prequel Novella

He's a rockstar, an artist, a fantasy who lives rent-free in Emily's head. And he's her roommate's best friend.

Robin is on top of the world, getting opportunities Emily can't even conceive, especially when she's focused on college and law school. It's easy for Robin to be nice to her, and easy for Emily to hide her crush when all they ever do is talk on the phone. When she finally meets Robin face-to-face, the fantasy -- and her crush -- takes on new proportions. But Robin lives in a different stratosphere. Nothing will ever come of Emily's crush. Right?

Read on for the first two chapters of

TAKE A CHANCE ON ME

CHAPTER ONE

WHEN JUSTIN ROLLED over, Vaughn made the move with him and landed astride his lap. Sunshine streaming around the edges of the window shades limned her silhouette with a goddess glow that heightened Justin's desire. She slid herself up his length, then down, pulling him into her and rubbing her pelvis against his. Justin exhaled and put both hands on her ass, squeezing as he pushed deeper.

Vaughn sat back, rocking her hips, and stretched. She reached forward, grabbed the antique metal headboard, and dangled her breasts over Justin's face. He lifted and captured one nipple with his mouth and teased it. Then he moved to her other breast and covered the one he had just kissed with his hand, rolling the nipple between his fingers.

Vaughn sat up again, put her hand over Justin's, and increased her rocking. She dropped her head back and sighed. "Ahh, Justin."

He sat up and ran his hands up and down her back, wanting to be closer as she pulsed around him.

He held her against him and searched for her mouth. When he caught her in a kiss, he groaned, basking in the feeling of her body's grip as he came.

She laughed against his mouth and gave one more firm thrust against him then pushed him down. She lay on his chest for a beat then rolled off, leaving one leg across his waist. "Good morning."

Justin held onto her leg, massaging her supple skin, and rolled to face her. "Yes, it is." With a hand in her hair, he pulled her to him and kissed her hard. "Miss me?" He had only been away a few weeks, but it'd felt longer to him.

Vaughn laughed again. "Never."

He smacked her ass, loving the ripple of her body against his. "Liar."

She kissed him then got out of the bed. "I'll never tell."

He smirked and watched her sashay into the bathroom, the ends of her newly colored hair forming a vee that pointed to her sweet ass. "I like the color you added. I would've expected black or bright red, but that dark wine color is sexy."

"Thanks." Vaughn stood in profile, her still erect nipples distracting him. "I figured since I was getting rid of the dishwater blonde, it should be a lot more interesting." She ran a hand through her straight locks, a glossy chestnut color with a burst of burgundy along her nape. "The under color gives it a pop."

Justin walked into the bathroom and smacked her ass again then turned his back to her as he removed and disposed of the condom. "Perfect for the bar owner seeking investors, who wants to keep her edge." He leaned over the bathtub and turned on the shower.

"Ugh. You went from hot booty call to sounding like my dad."

Justin laughed and climbed in the shower. "Great minds."

"Whatever." She pulled the shower curtain back and joined him.

Head under the stream of water, Justin grabbed her wrist when she slapped a bar of soap against his chest. He held onto her, lowered his head, and kissed her, pulling her against his semi. Vaughn always appealed to him but with water running over her lush body? Irresistible.

"Already?"

"I'm not afraid to admit I missed you." His voice was hoarse.

Vaughn hugged him then stepped back. "Not now, Sparky, I've got a banker to meet."

He groaned. He didn't necessarily need sex, but he wanted that connection with her again—damn near craved it. "What if I'm fast?"

"You're never fast. Especially not in the shower. That's why I like you." She spun them around and put herself under the water.

"Fine." He handed her a bottle of shampoo. She was right. He did like to savor her when they showered together. Everywhere, really. The only time quickies interested him was that first romp after he'd been away for a while. But when it was time for round two? That took a good while. They both liked it that way. He knew because after his most recent homecoming, Vaughn had reached for him first after they had taken the edge off.

They traded spots again, and Justin rinsed off. "Need help shaving?"

"I got it under control, Just."

He squeezed her ass, kissed her neck, and stepped out of the shower. He pulled a towel from the rack nearby and dried off. "Wanna grab lunch after the banker?"

"Um, maybe." The knob squeaked as Vaughn adjusted the temperature. She made a noise as though she'd been doused with a bucket of cold water and turned off the shower a few seconds later.

"Why do you always do that?"

"Do what?" She took the fresh towel Justin offered.

"That shot of cold water. It sounds like you suffer through it every time."

She finished drying her legs and wrapped the towel around herself, securing it between her breasts. "Beauty is suffering, Justin."

"Chicks are weird."

She pulled the towel from his waist and cracked it against his ass before re-hanging it.

He rubbed the spot she'd hit and grinned. She'd said no to another round of sex, but she was still playful. He liked it and was tempted to show her how much. But he figured her meeting was important, so he went to the bedroom, found his pants, and pulled them on. "Any idea where my shirt might be?"

"Look between the couch and the kitchen," Vaughn called from the bathroom.

He checked the living room, finding his phone wedged between the couch cushions. He picked it up, continued to the kitchen and got a glass of water, then started a pot of coffee as he thumbed through the alerts.

He had a missed call from Sue Douglas, his close friend and the PR genius for his band, Words Fail Me. He listened to her voicemail then sent her a quick text. When she responded a moment later, he called her.

"Hey, Sexy Sue, what's going on?"

"You know I'm flying in today, right?"

"Yep. When do I get to see you?" Justin chugged some water.

"Sooner than I'd planned," Sue said. "Well, I hope sooner."

"What's going on?"

"Our usually reliable band manager talked me out of renting a car, and now he can't pick me up. I tried to reserve one online, but they say they only have minivans."

Justin set a mug on the counter next to the brewing coffee pot. "We can't even use that to go to a gig." Minivans were great for moving gear or people, but not all their gear and people at the same time.

"I know. Hang on." A garbled announcement overpowered Sue. "Okay, Adam flies in tomorrow, and he has a rental, but I need a pickup in Detroit today. Can you do it? I can get a cab when I land, but I'd rather buy you lunch."

"When do you get in?"

"About three hours."

Justin plucked a caramel from the half empty Halloween bowl on the counter, crinkling the wrapper, then popped the candy in his mouth. Halloween already? He checked the date and time—shit, October already—and read his schedule, which was empty until the evening when he and Brad, his best friend and the band's lead singer, would meet at the recording studio to listen to the tracks they'd laid down over the last few days. "Yeah, I can do that."

"Later, Sexy Sue." Justin disconnected the call and got the milk from the refrigerator.

"Sexy Sue?" Vaughn tossed Justin's shirt at him then beelined for the coffeepot. She hovered over it, taking deep breaths. She was so addicted to coffee that despite the chill in the apartment, she only wore her bra and panties, with a towel still wrapped around her hair. She wouldn't finish getting dressed until she drank half a cup. On the rare occasion when there wasn't coffee to brew, Justin would take her to her favorite coffee shop, pretending it was a real date— the downside to his "hot booty call" status being that Vaughn refused to let him take her out for breakfast. She used her night owl schedule as a bartender as her reason, but it had started to feel more like an excuse.

"Yeah, I told you about Sue. She got us on *The Tonight Show*. She's flying in to work on promos for the new album."

"Still." Vaughn faced him and leaned against the counter. "Not many guys call a chick ten minutes after they banged another one. And while they're still half naked to boot." She made an obvious show of dragging her gaze down his bare chest.

Justin grinned and handed Vaughn the small jug of milk then caged her in his arms against the counter. "Last night you said you like me naked."

"Oh, I do." Vaughn didn't back down as Justin grazed his lips up her neck and past her mouth. "I especially like how you make me coffee when we're done fucking."

Justin pulled back enough to look Vaughn in the eye. "Is that all this is?"

"Isn't it?" Vaughn turned in his arms and poured the coffee into the mug Justin had left out.

He pulled on his shirt then kissed her temple and rolled his shoulders back. He honestly didn't know what it was between them. He'd spent two weeks in Brazil for his bandmate Darryl's wedding, and in between amazing sight-seeing and the epic reception, all he could think about was getting back to Vaughn. Even that had to wait. He'd spent his first three days home in the recording studio with Brad and Chris, the rest of the band. When they ran out of new ideas to record, he didn't even think. He drove straight to Vaughn's bar. Now that he'd be home for a while, he planned to explore his feelings for her and whether she felt the same.

Justin walked through the apartment. He found his shoes between the coffee table and Vaughn's bedroom. "Can I see you before you go to work tonight?" His keys lay on the floor next to the front door.

"I don't know. What're you doing with Sexy Sue?" Vaughn raised her eyebrows when she said the word sexy.

Justin grimaced. It figured—out of the whole conversation, that's the part Vaughn would hear and remember. "Brad gave her that nickname." He put special emphasis on Brad's name. "It's strictly business. I'm picking her up from the airport, possibly grabbing a burger. and talking about the album. No big deal."

"Call me after burgers."

"You should come with us." Justin fished in his pockets for an elastic then pulled his damp hair into a low ponytail. "You two have a lot in common."

"Hard pass." Vaughn bristled as she set down her coffee. "Besides, I probably won't get out of this meeting before two. We can hook up later."

"Okay." He wanted Vaughn to meet Sue, see that the only things between them were hard work and friendship, but more than that, he wanted more time with Vaughn. Maybe he could arrange a meeting between the two women at the coffee shop Vaughn liked. Justin returned to the kitchen and leaned against the sink. "When did you move the table away from the door?"

"While you were on tour."

Justin shook his head. "Nope. That's where I left my shirt last time."

Vaughn's cheeks pinked. She must've remembered how her roommate came home that night and screamed when she saw the T-shirt, thinking something bad had happened. "That's right." She sipped her coffee. "Must've been when you were in Brazil. You weren't here when Marnie broke up with her boyfriend, right?"

"Right."

"Yeah, he kinda slammed his way out when she ended things. I moved the table to save it."

Justin put a hand on Vaughn's hip. "Did he slam you or Marnie?" He loved traveling and having new experiences, but he hated that bad shit could happen when he was away, and he couldn't do anything about it. Vaughn ran a bar. That situation was ripe for bad shit.

She softened toward him. "No. He wasn't a jerk or anything. Just melodramatic."

"Good." Justin pulled her toward him and wrapped his arms around her. She was warm and soft, fresh from the shower and velvety from the honey scented lotion she used. "You should've come to Brazil with me. Darryl's wedding was awesome."

"And keep you from Brazilian pussy? Never."

He forced a smile despite the sting her words delivered and kissed her. "There isn't a woman in Brazil who can hold a candle to you." In fact, he'd yet to meet a woman anywhere who could outshine Vaugh. He hadn't even been looking. It took the wedding to make him realize it. That she encouraged him to experience other women burned on multiple levels and forced him to consider whether she had another guy, or guys, waiting in the wings. He saw the way men looked at her. Vaughn had more than a few admirers.

"Friends with benefits aren't supposed to get sappy." She kissed his cheek then stepped out of his embrace, pulling the towel off her hair.

"What if I want more?" He'd been dying to ask her this question since the end of their European tour a few months ago. She'd been the first person he saw when he got home, and while she'd obviously been happy to see him and took him home that night, she held him at arm's length. He needed that to stop. He didn't want to freak her out, though. They'd met right as Words Fail Me had gotten their first big break and wound up being casual for a few years.

"You stick around town for more than a season, and that might happen." She walked toward her bedroom.

Justin followed and goosed her. "Is that all it takes? I give up my nomadic life?"

"Maybe."

He pulled her into another embrace, trying to remove the distance her shrug had put between them and taking comfort from her settling into his arms. "Or you can come with me. You might like seeing the world with me."

117

Vaughn ducked her head and chuckled. "Sure, rock star." She pushed on his shoulder. "Go see your publicist."

He tightened his hug and kissed her forehead. He needed to figure out how to express his feelings. He was into her, and not just for the sake of beating out other townies. He'd never felt comfortable asking her to be exclusive when there were times when he didn't know when he'd be able to call her, let alone come home. The tour that had just ended had been extended twice, with Darryl's wedding quickly following. He needed a strategy before he kicked this into high gear so he wouldn't scare her away.

"Fine. I'm giving you an easy out. Don't be surprised when I bring it up again."

"Okay." Vaughn gave him a light kiss. "Get out of here. I have to make sure my stuff is ready for the bank."

Justin let her go and backed toward the door. "Let me know how it goes."

"I will."

He stopped with his hand on the knob. "I mean it!"

"I will text you as soon as the meeting is over."

"All right." Justin winked. "Good luck." He meant it. Whether they were an on again off again fling, or something more, Vaughn was good people. He wanted to see her achieve her goals.

Vaughn ran her hand through her hair and smiled. "Thanks, Just."

CHAPTER TWO

VAUGHN PULLED INTO the bank parking lot and left the motor running for the heat. She checked her reflection in the mirror, running a finger under her lip to smooth her lipstick. She pushed her fingers against the bottom of her chin—the point of her heart-shaped face the same as Maeve's—and sighed. "I look like my mother." She slid the door closed and flipped up the visor.

"Who is stunning." Her dad somehow sounded both stern and supportive when he spoke. "It could be much worse. You could look like me."

Vaughn gave a soft laugh as she switched the phone from her car's Bluetooth to the handset. "Looking like you would not be a hardship, Dad." Her father was the most handsome man in the world, and she told him that often. She truly believed it, but neither of them hung their esteem on their looks. In fact, resembling Maeve wouldn't usually bother Vaughn. Today, it tormented her.

"That's what you think, but I bet my face wouldn't make the tips you do."

That got a genuine laugh from Vaughn. Her dad had been in the bar when she worked. He saw the no-nonsense expression she gave all her customers, save a few regulars and Justin. She couldn't live off tips from that crowd.

"Is your face calling me from home or the office?" Vaughn asked, changing the subject.

"The office. I had an early root canal."

Vaughn grimaced then checked her teeth in the rearview mirror. She'd been in her dad's dental office often enough when people left with swollen mouths that she was meticulous with her teeth. "Did you tell Maeve about today?"

"You can still call her Mom, and you asked me not to, so I didn't. She'd be really proud, though."

"You sure about that?"

"Positive."

Vaughn's mother was a gifted accountant and had taught her everything about money. As a result, Vaughn's business plan covered every financial aspect of the new bar she planned to open and how she'd repay the loan. Her current location, Crawford's, was profitable, which meant even in lean months, she wouldn't struggle to make the payments on the loan for a new place. She was proud of that and hoped it would strengthen her application. But she wouldn't share any of that information with Maeve. The woman had made it clear when Vaughn started college that she thought Vaughn taking over her grandfather's bar wasn't "ladylike," and Vaughn was "too smart" to spend her time "dealing with drunks."

She remembered the moment she learned exactly how much her mother was against her with unflinching clarity. It had been a week after her grandfather's funeral. Maeve had asked Vaughn to go with her to the office to pick up paperwork. Vaughn hadn't expected her uncle and an attorney to be there, or to learn that Cil had left Crawford's to *her*, not Maeve or Uncle Lorcan.

Maeve had directed her into the room where everyone waited, made her sit, and then perched on the edge of the desk while the attorney explained the inheritance. The moment the man stopped speaking, Maeve pounced.

"Sweetie, I know this is a lot. But we have a plan."

"What plan?" Vaughn had asked. She'd officially been on staff at the bar for two years and running it with the general manager-in-training for six months. Being an owner operator didn't scare her. But she worried that her uncle might be insulted. The bar had long been a point of contention between Uncle Lori and Cil. Did he want it?

"I asked Lori to buy the bar."

Vaughn turned to her uncle. She wouldn't stand in his way if he wanted Crawford's, but she hoped he'd let her continue to work there. "You want it?"

Uncle Lori hesitated before he answered. "If you want Crawford's to stay in the family, I'll buy it."

"I'm not sure what that means."

Maeve gave Vaughn a placating smile. "It means you don't have to worry about the bar. You can go to graduate school or explore other jobs. You can do whatever you want."

"But I love Crawford's."

"We know," Uncle Lori said. "And if you want it to stay in the family, maybe take it later, I'll hang on to it for you."

"Hang on to it? I want it, but do you?"

Uncle Lori shifted, his discomfort clear. "Crawford's was Dad's dream."

"If you don't want it, why are you offering to buy it?"

Maeve smiled and squeezed Vaughn's hand. "To give you freedom. To let you find work you're truly suited for."

Vaughn reared back, pulling her hand away. "What?"

"A bar isn't a place for a young woman. You have so many options. My father is tying you down. Uncle Lori is offering you freedom."

Vaughn sat in silence, blinking as she tried to rein in her anger before she said something she might regret. She let her brain sift and sort all the news into place. Then she addressed her uncle. "Be honest. Do you want Crawford's?"

He shook his head.

"You made this offer because *she* asked you to." Vaughn jerked a thumb toward Maeve.

"Yes."

Vaughn whipped her glare at Maeve. "What the fuck, Mom?"

"Why do you have to be so coarse? This is exactly why you need options."

"Are either of you upset that Cil skipped over you and gave me the bar?" If this was a case of either her mom or uncle feeling cheated, she'd make it right.

"No, you love the bar more than anyone," Uncle Lori said.

"Mom?"

"You should have your own dream."

"Crawford's is my dream!" Vaughn stood, feeling like a caged animal. She'd long known her mother worried that Cil had pushed the bar on her, but it had always been the opposite. She'd always wanted to be at Crawford's, had dreamed of being a bartender, and eventually, of being in charge. She didn't understand why it was so difficult for her mother to grasp.

"What young woman dreams of hosing vomit off the sidewalk in front of her business and dealing with roughnecks?"

"Oh my God, Mom. Seriously?"

"It's not the right life for you."

She took a step closer to Maeve. "I'm an adult. I get to decide that."

"Vaughn, use some sense."

Blood pounded against Vaughn's temples. All she wanted to do was scream in frustration. "I can't have this conversation right now." She tried to smile at the attorney who'd been silent through their conversation. "Do you need to finalize paperwork today?"

"No."

"Perfect. I can't do this with *her* here." Vaughn glared at Maeve again. "Do you have a card?"

The attorney gave her a folder with his card stapled to it. "For your review. Let me know what you decide."

"Thank you." She stormed out of Maeve's office and hadn't been back since. She told her father what had happened, and he'd been angry on her behalf. He'd known about the plan but didn't realize Maeve would spring it on Vaughn.

Uncle Lori flew back to Spokane the next week and Vaughn signed the papers making her the new owner of Crawford's. Maeve had left countless voicemails arguing the point, rife with insults toward the bar. When the calls went unanswered, Maeve resorted to sending so many emails that Vaughn blocked her.

The encounter had struck deep. Cil had started Crawford's, and her mother and uncle had both worked there over the years. When Cil suffered a stroke then got a bout of pneumonia that hospitalized him and took months of recovery, Vaughn's parents moved their little family from steamy Miami, Florida to Ann Arbor, forcing her father to start a new dental practice while Maeve and Uncle Lori kept the bar open. Vaughn's first job had been doing inventory at Crawford's. But at the first opportunity, Maeve had been ready to bury the bar, right alongside Cil.

Vaughn pushed away the anger that memories of Maeve's scheming always brought up. "You know how she feels about my business."

"And I know how she feels about *you*. She's impressed, Vaughn. She doesn't express it well, but she wants you to have every success."

"Yep. Every success that doesn't involve owning and operating a bar." Vaughn banged her head back against her seat.

"Are you sure you want to discuss this right now? Aren't you about to present to the bank?"

"You're right. I should focus. Get in the zone." Vaughn opened the mirror again and smoothed her hair.

"You're gonna be great. Your presentation is fantastic. I've never seen a better practice session."

Instead of pouring over the loan application and the accompanying presentation with Maeve, Vaughn had done most of the work alone. After running the numbers and carefully building her presentation, she'd practiced in front of her roommate and best friend, Marnie, and again with Gusty, one of the regulars at Crawford's. The older man had taken great pleasure in sitting behind Cil's desk in the bar office. But he'd grilled her, demanding answers to all the questions he'd faced when he'd applied for his own business loan.

He'd been hard on her, and it was worth it. By the time Vaughn did her final run through with her dad, she'd felt more prepared than ever. It would've been nice to call Maeve for one last check, but she'd gotten used to not talking shop with her anymore.

"Thanks, Dad. Maeve always encouraged practicing. And I like feeling prepared." Her mother was a smart woman and giving her credit wasn't hard to do, but it still stung. Maeve had groomed her for success, and Vaughn would never share it with her.

"She gives a lot of top-notch advice."

Vaughn sighed. Sooner or later, they'd have to fight this out. Her dad constantly tried to bridge the rift between the two women, but it wasn't getting fixed today. "Maeve's right about all kinds of things, and I admire that. It's her misogyny I have a problem with."

Now her dad sighed. "It's not misogyny."

Vaughn pressed a hand against her eyes. "Another time, Dad. I have to get in there."

"I love you, and I'm proud of you no matter what."

"Love you, Dad. I'll call later." Vaughn hung up and dropped the phone in her purse. She turned off the car and got out, reaching into the backseat for her blazer. As she buttoned the black wool, she shook off thoughts of her parents and focused on all the prep she'd done. She smiled as she gathered her printed materials—they were excellent—and turned toward the bank.

A young man in a sweater vest with an "assistant" badge greeted her when she entered. The main room of the bank was trendy and open like a computer store, but as soon as she turned into the hallway leading to the conference rooms, it was all old school institution. Thick carpet that smelled freshly cleaned dulled the sound of her steps, and framed stock certificates and historical photos lined the walls. As she made her way, she noticed a placard outside an office with the name "Susan." She resisted the urge to roll her eyes. The last thing she needed was another reminder of "Sexy Sue."

Her relationship with Justin had always been blissfully casual, but his timing when he called that woman was...not the best. In fact, Vaughn had hated overhearing the conversation. She knew who Sue was and believed Justin when he said their relationship was platonic. She shouldn't even care. Justin did whatever he did when he was on tour. And when he was home, he was with Vaughn. She'd always been fine with that. Even when he left, and she had to take a few days to adjust to not getting regular texts from him asking when he could see her.

It shouldn't matter, anyway. When she got approved for this loan, she'd be too busy remodeling the new space, hiring and training new staff, and launching her mixology curriculum. Justin had never been more than a temporary pleasure. Him calling some woman didn't change that.

Turning into the conference room, Vaughn got another hit of institutional banking: a long cherry conference table, high back leather chairs. A scent like tobacco lingered, though smoking in buildings like this had been banned long ago. She smiled. After years of hearing business people talk in Crawford's, Vaughn knew she could handle this.

"Can I get you a drink?" The assistant's words snapped Vaughn back to reality. "We have water, coffee, and several sodas."

"No, thank you."

"The Wi-Fi password is on the card next to the wires." He pointed to a hub of different colored cords on a credenza at the front of the room. "Can I help you set up?"

"Actually, a glass of water would be great." Vaughn went to work, attaching her computer to the projector and setting out the materials she'd prepared. She quietly thanked Justin for taking her mind off her parents and then the assistant for taking her mind off Justin.

She finished arranging her materials as several people filed into the room and gave them each a warm smile as they introduced themselves. She flipped open the small notebook she'd brought to look prepared. She'd remember anything they asked her without having to write it down. In the lower left margin was a little stick figure drawing that looked like her behind her bar and a note.

You're smooth like 30-year-old Macallan. Can't wait to celebrate your new biz. -J

Vaughn smiled then started her presentation, hoping she'd have good news to share with Justin when she was done. Celebrating with him was always fun.